I0537654

Winter Formal

A Southern College Novella

By Meda White

Winter Formal
Copyright © 2014 Meda White

Editor: Andrea Grimm
Cover Artist: Kari Ayasha, Cover to Cover Designs

ISBN: 1941287042
ISBN-13: 978-1-941287-04-0

DEDICATION

To Papa Boyd,
Thank you for your support, encouragement, the press releases, and the boiled peanuts.
Love Always,
Your Number One Non-Son

ACKNOWLEDGMENTS

In loving memory of Comer Marshall Hunt
9/20/77 – 12/11/77
Thank you to my big ole family for sharing your talent
and cheering me on—aunts, uncles, cousins, in-laws,
and out-laws. I love y'all.

To the Brooks Family- in loving memory of Sylvia
"Sibba" Brooks Larson. I consider you all part of my
extended family. Thanks for adopting me into your big,
loving clan. Much love and many blessings.

Chapter One

Sibba Douglas opened the flap of her messenger bag and gasped. Her upper lip started sweating as she drew the bag closer to her body and away from Mike Ferguson, M.D. Maybe concealing the drug paraphernalia would make him unsee it.

"What's the matter?" Dr. Ferguson had a twinkle in his eye.

Sibba took a step back. "Nothing. It's just...I mean...I forgot my intern hours sheet. I'll bring it by next week so you can sign off for me."

Her sweaty hands slid on the strap of her bag. "Thanks again for letting me get my volunteer hours in your office, Doc. It's been a great experience."

"I'm glad you think so." The doctor turned to go and then paused. "I wonder if I can ask a favor?"

Her heart was in her throat. *Oh, God. If I say no, he'll rat me out.* "Yes, sir?"

"My godson is going to do his hours with me, if he can ever find the time. He's not doing very well in his sciences. I'm worried he won't be prepared for the MCAT in January."

Sibba swallowed, wondering what the favor was. Did he want her to take the test for his godson? Because she wouldn't do that. It was immoral. Unethical. Illegal. Like having a marijuana pipe in her messenger bag.

Oh, God. He might call the cops. Or worse, my dad. Her heart pummeled against her sternum.

"I was wondering if you could tutor him? His father and I grew up together in New York, so I've known him all his life. He's a good kid, just over-committed."

"Ah, yeah. Sure. I can do that." A bead of sweat ran from her hairline down to her jaw.

"Are you okay, Sibba?" He stepped toward her and put a hand on her arm.

She backed up. "Yes, sir. Fine. Just give him my number, and we'll set something up. Thanks again. See ya later."

She bolted for the back door. Once inside her rusting Mustang, which she'd cleverly named Rusty, she rested her forehead on the steering wheel and groaned.

Doc didn't say anything, but he had to have seen it. He was right beside her. How could anyone have missed the colorful blown glass pipe? It was possible he didn't know what it was for.

She beat her head against the wheel again.

Except, she was sure he did. He was a medical doctor. It was her goal to be a doctor someday, too. Preferably somewhere far away from the Southeastern U.S.; she wanted to see the world.

She wouldn't achieve her goals if she got caught with bud. She'd already promised herself she'd quit as soon as she got her acceptance letter from medical school. The urge to adjust the timetable was strong. But, the urge to burn one was stronger.

It would have to wait until she got home, as she wasn't in the habit of carrying it around. The pipe was a gift from her friend, Jon-Jon. He stopped by her place about once a week to check in, catch up, and annoy her roommate, Finlee. She should just give her stash to her roomie and be done with it.

A knock at her window made her jump and scream. Seeing it was the nurse, she rolled down her window.

"I'm taking the lab coats home to wash and noticed you forgot to leave yours."

Sibba looked down at the white coat she still wore. "Oh gosh, I'm sorry." She got out of the car and removed the jacket.

The nurse took it. "Don't hold your breath for that boy to call."

Sibba furrowed her brow. "What boy?"

"The godson."

She'd already forgotten. Her brain was fried. What started in high school as a way to have a little fun had become a habit. She was getting off the herb...for good.

***

The page from his textbook stuck to his forehead when Nash Lincoln tried to sit up to answer his phone. He'd fallen asleep studying again. He rubbed his hand across his face before he looked at the display.

"Uncle Mike, you caught me with my head in a book."

"I'm glad to hear it. Listen, I found you a tutor. I'll text her number to you, but I want you to promise me you'll call and set up a time to meet with her. She's super smart."

Nash groaned. "I've got study buddies here at the house. I can get help if I need it."

"You need it. Trust me, Nash, the MCAT is no joke."

"If I screw up the first time, I can take it again."

"You have to do well every time, in case your school of choice looks at all your scores. You know how much this means to your parents."

Nash sighed and scratched the stubble on his chin. "All right. Send her number."

He hung up and checked the time. He needed to finish his assignment before the guys knocked on his door for the weekly house meeting. If he weren't the vice-president of I Grabda Thi, he'd skip it. He was also chairing the planning committee for Winter Formal, and it was a topic on the agenda. That and the charity clay shoot he was also helping plan. Being from New York, he'd never seen the appeal in hunting and shooting, but in South Alabama, it was a way of life. He was glad to head it up because it meant he wouldn't actually have to participate and be emasculated by his inability to hit the flying targets.

After the meeting, they'd go out to the Passing Grade and get hammered. Thursday night was

4

ladies night, and their sorority friends would buy them cheap drinks as long as they danced.

He opened the drawer of his desk and pulled out the plastic sandwich baggie. He was almost out of Bennies, and he needed them more now than ever, since it was early October and midterms were the following week. They helped him focus, and they weren't illegal drugs, so it wasn't like they'd give him brain damage or anything. Thousands of kids took Ritalin and Adderall for ADHD every day.

His phone dinged and he glanced at the screen. "Thanks a lot, Uncle Mike. Pile it on."

There was a number without a name, so he entered it in his contacts as Super-smart Girl.

He took a Vitamin R and an Addie out of the bag and chased them with the Monster energy drink sweating on his desk. One used to be enough, but he was building up a tolerance and needed more to get the same effects.

He bent his head back to his assignment.

A little later, the door opened and his roommate, Laith, came in. "Hey, bro. Almost time for the meeting."

Laith dropped his backpack on his bed and removed his T-shirt. He used the shirt to wipe under his arms before tossing it in the hamper. Then he applied deodorant and cologne before he put on a clean shirt.

Nash shook his head. Laith had the Latino thing going for him, and the girls were crazy about him. It didn't hurt that he was also a nice guy, but most of the brothers were.

Brothers. Nash still had a hard time accepting the terminology. It wouldn't have been a problem if his real brother hadn't died when they were teens. He shook off the depressing thought about the time his heart rate picked up, and his skin started to warm. *Good.* The pills were working.

Nash stood to change his own shirt.

"Dude, are you losing weight on purpose?" Laith asked. "Your pants are about to fall off."

Nash looked down at his jeans slung lower on his hips than usual. He was on the verge of the underwear revealing trend popular with prison inmates as a sign of availability. A shiver ran over him before he reached for a belt.

"I'm gonna buy you some suspenders. I don't wanna see your drawers."

Nash smiled. Laith's parents were Mexican immigrants, but he was a self-proclaimed redneck, and it showed in his speech.

"Too busy to eat. You know how it is."

"Naw, man, I don't." Laith flexed his biceps. "Gotta feed the machine."

Nash shook his head and checked his schedule for Friday before he sent a text to the super-smart tutor Uncle Mike had hooked him up with. In it, he let her know he had a two-hour window on Friday. It was that or nothing. Hopefully, she couldn't make it, and he could at least say he'd tried.

Chapter Two

Sibba was in the process of handing all drug related paraphernalia over to Finlee when a text came through from the godson.

"Ugh, I was hoping he wouldn't be interested in my help." She entered him in her contacts as Godson and texted saying she'd meet him at the library at two. She was glad he had limited availability. That way it would be on him if she couldn't help him, and Dr. Ferguson would have to stop blackmailing her.

"I think you're overreacting." Finlee turned the glass pipe over in her hands. "But, I do love this. Are you sure he saw it?"

"I don't see how he could've missed it." She'd already demonstrated how they were standing and how close he was when the life-changing event occurred. "I just hope he'll keep quiet as long as I do his favor. An arrest would ruin my life."

"Not to mention, your dad would bury you

under the jail."

Her dad was the Chief of Police in their small hometown, and he had a zero tolerance policy for illegal drug use. He'd secretly wanted to work for the DEA, but when he found out her mom was pregnant with her and her brother, they'd gotten married and stayed put to be near their families.

"Okay. I get it." Finlee took a rolling paper out of the package. "You were going to quit soon anyway." She put the dried leaves on the folded paper and spread them out. "My uncle is gonna wonder why it's taking us longer to use our stash." She rolled the joint and licked the edge to seal it closed. "But, just in case. I'll leave this here with Jack." She placed it in the mouth of the Jack-O-Lantern they'd carved as practice for Halloween. "You get stressed, you come see Jack."

The temptation was already too much, but she needed to focus. Sibba patted the top of the big orange vegetable. "Enjoy, Jack."

Finlee stood and turned toward her room. "Go change, my drug-free friend. It's ladies' night."

Sibba didn't see the need to dress up to go to a bar. She wasn't interested in any of the country boys who'd be there. She was waiting to manhunt until she got to medical school up north. In general, Southern boys were good guys, but she wanted to broaden her horizons and explore other cultures. It was a big world out there.

***

At the bar, a hefty guy named Eddie took Finlee's chair when she got up to dance. Sibba spent the next half hour reminding him she was the designated driver every time he offered to buy her a drink. Just when she was trying to explain to him the irony of naming a college bar the Passing Grade, her savior arrived.

"How's my girl?" He bent and kissed her head.

"Jon-Jon. Where've you been hiding?" She stood and hugged her old friend from high school. He was a year ahead, but they were from a small school where everyone knew everyone.

"Here and there. Are you still a genius?" He took the seat Eddie vacated.

"I'm not a genius. I study hard."

"I know you do." He pinched her cheek. "But I think you got extra brain cells to go with the extra hair follicles God gave you."

Her hand flew to her curls. She'd been cursed with naturally kinky hair. It was the bane of her existence, requiring much effort and product to keep it under control.

Before she could respond, a hot guy tapped Jon-Jon's shoulder. "Hey, I need to talk to you."

Jon-Jon kissed the back of her hand before he stood. "I'll see you later, kiddo." He walked away, but the guy lingered and stared a minute.

Sibba shifted in her seat and adjusted her glasses as she looked for Finlee on the dance floor. When she turned back, he was gone.

***

Nash set his cup down on the hood of a car off to the side of the dirt and gravel parking lot and wiped his hands on his pants. The cool night air helped clear his head and cool his body. He was sweating like crazy.

He turned to his fraternity brother, who was also his supplier and hoped he couldn't see well in the dim light. "Who was the girl you were talking to?"

"No one you need to worry about." Jon-Jon sipped his beer and wiped the foam from his lip. "Stay away from her."

Nash didn't care. Not really. But he was curious about her, had been for a while. He decided to let it go and get down to business. "Do you have any R-balls or Black Beauties?"

"No, man. I'm waiting on a new supply. Have you ever tried Red Devils?"

Nash thought for a moment and shook his head.

Jon-Jon reached into his pocket and pulled out a coin envelope. He opened it and poured two pills into his hand. "It's over-the-counter cold medicine, but has similar effects to the others. Try these, and if you like it, I can get more without it going into the system."

"What system?"

"If you try to buy it, the pharmacy scans your I.D., and it goes into the system. It's supposed to keep you from buying a large quantity."

"Why would anyone need a large quantity?"

"You haven't learned much in your years here, have you?" Jon-Jon crossed his arms. "People use it to make meth."

"Oh." Nash examined the pills in his open palm.

Amphetamines. Methamphetamines. They were kissing cousins, as Laith would say.

Nash had drank too much while waiting for Jon-Jon to arrive, and his stomach was cramping and his chest felt funny. He wasn't sure he should take them now. His brain was already having trouble keeping up.

Jon-Jon didn't say anything, but he crossed his arms and leaned against the car, applying pressure whether he intended to or not.

Nash lifted his cup of cheap draft beer to make sure he had enough to chase the pills before he threw them in the back of his throat. His gag reflex kicked in, but he made himself swallow.

"Good man." Jon-Jon slapped him on the back. "Come on. Let's go back in and get another drink. I might let you look at my friend. She's your girl-next-door type. Sweet and smart."

"Tempting, but I think I'll wait out here a minute. Fresh air and all." Nash leaned against an old sports car and dropped his head back to look at the stars.

He did like the South. It was peaceful. And this time of year, the climate was agreeable. Even in winter, he barely needed more than a barn jacket. He'd nearly gotten laughed out of his fraternity house when he'd tried to wear his wool overcoat the first January he was here. In the city, he would've fit right in.

He smiled at the memory, but it got fuzzy and he rubbed his fist against a pain in his chest. A burp relieved some of the pressure, but he shivered at the awful taste that filled his mouth. His stomach was unsettled.

The next thing he knew, gravel dug into his

palms. He tried to lift his head, but it was too heavy. He was on his hands and knees, but with a huge effort, he pushed himself onto his butt and leaned against the car. That was when the world went black.

Chapter Three

"Hey, hippie chick."

Sibba turned to see Eddie approaching. She looked for an escape, but the building was over capacity, and she couldn't get away fast enough. "I'm not a hippie."

"I didn't mean it bad." He slurred. "But, you don't brush your hair, and you're wearing that…" He pointed. "What kind of skirt is that anyway?"

It was a broomstick skirt, but after the dig on her locks, she wasn't in the mood to accommodate him with a fashion lesson. "It's Bohemian."

She spotted Finlee coming her way. It was after midnight, which was the time they'd agreed to leave unless Finlee found another ride. "Hey, girlfriend. You ready?"

Sibba nodded and waved goodbye to Eddie as she made her way to the door. Once outside, she inhaled and wrapped her sweater tighter around her upper half. Since she was cold most of the time, long sweaters were a way of life. They also helped disguise her less bony lower half.

She pulled her keys from her pocket and walked around the front of her car where she nearly stepped on a guy. His chin rested on his chest at an odd angle, so she bent down to check for a pulse.

He had one, but it was what Dr. Ferguson called thready.

She took his face in her hands and popped his cheek lightly. "Hey. Are you okay?"

A groan was all she got in response. She thought about calling an ambulance, but then saw the vomit on the ground next to the guy. "Hey, are you better since you vomited?"

He opened his eyes and looked at her and then the ground. "Not my puke."

Finlee came around the back of the car. "Gross. Who puked right next to Rusty?"

"This guy, I think."

His eyes were closed again, but he mumbled something that sounded like, "Not my puke."

"Fin, should we go in and find someone who knows him?"

"Who is he?"

"I don't know." She held his face up toward the security light. "I think Jon-Jon knows him."

"Well, you know I'm not going to find him. Let's just prop this guy on another car and go."

"I can't just leave him unattended. What if he gets sick again and aspirates on his own fluids."

"Stop it. No doctor talk, or I'll defecate to add to his pile here."

Sibba laughed. "You mean regurgitate. I

wouldn't want you dropping a deuce here in the parking lot."

"What did I say? Never mind, I'm drunk and I'm going to law school, not medical school. Let's go home."

Sibba let go of the guy's face, and it lolled forward. He wasn't so hot, wasted next to the contents of his stomach. "Get in the car and wait for me. I'll run in real quick to look for Jon-Jon."

She made a pass around the perimeter of the bar, but didn't find anyone who could help. Back at the car, she stood over the semi-conscious guy and debated her options. "Finlee, help me get him in the car."

"What are you gonna do, Sib? Drive him to the Greek Village and dump him in the front yard of one of the houses for someone to find?"

"How do you know he's a frat boy?"

"Look at him. Button-up tucked into belted jeans. Preppy country boy equals fraternity affiliation."

"I told you he can't be left alone. We'll take him home with us, and I can check on him during the night."

"Are you crazy? What if he's an insane rapist killer?"

"He can't even hold his head up. How's he gonna kill us?"

"Maybe it's a ruse. When we get him home, he'll jump us."

"If he does, then we'll put him down with one of our three handguns, four shotguns, or two rifles. You can choose the weapon."

"Oh, all right." Finlee huffed as she marched over to help get him up.

Sibba felt a strain in her lower back when she lifted him. She was in an awkward stance to avoid stepping in the vomit. "He's heavier than he looks."

"Yeah, I don't think we can get him in and out of the back seat." Finlee sighed. "I guess I'll ride in the back. He better be grateful for this."

Sibba struggled to buckle the seatbelt for her comatose passenger before she turned the key and headed for the country. She shared a trailer with Finlee just outside the city. Finlee's dad, who was a big time cattle farmer, had gotten it for them. Her uncle was another kind of farmer, and everyone in the county they grew up in knew it. Sibba's dad had struggled in vain for years to keep his little girl from being best friends with Finlee Sanders.

At home, when they deposited John Doe onto Sibba's bed, Finlee said, "My turn to pass out. Yell if he attacks you."

Sibba took his shoes off and left him to go get a bucket and washcloths, in case he got sick again. It took her a few minutes to empty the bucket of the cleaning supplies and rinse it out. When she returned to her room, the bucket slipped from her hand and bounced off the wood floor.

Stretched out on her bed was a naked man. Buck naked. She'd taken anatomy classes, but they hadn't prepared her for this. It occurred to her he might do exactly what Finlee imagined, but she dismissed the idea when a snore escaped from him.

He was on his back with one arm over his face and his business on display. Curiosity made her take a step closer. It was like observing an animal in the wild. A sleeping, naked animal. In the lamp light, the hair on his head was dark. She would've guessed brown, but everything else, from the stubble on his face to far-reaching places, was ginger.

He was slim, but muscular, especially his torso. He probably did push-ups and crunches every day.

She made herself stop ogling the poor guy when she realized she was fantasizing about touching his smooth skin to feel the hard muscle beneath.

She put the bucket on the table next to the bed and almost sat next to him before she caught herself. "Hey, I'll check on you later. Holler if you need something."

He didn't budge. She took one last look and let out a long breath before she reached for a blanket to cover him. When she got to the door and looked back, he rolled over and the blanket landed on the floor.

Her body reacted unexpectedly as heat flooded from her core in every direction. Physiologically, she knew what was happening to her. Hormones. Psychologically, she was rattled. "I cannot unsee that."

Chapter Four

Nash rolled over and grunted when he opened his eyes. The room was bright so he shut his eyes again, trying to hold onto the remnants of a dream about his brother. Chad had been trying to tell him something, but he couldn't understand it so he gave up.

He didn't know what was worse, the pain in his head or the taste in his mouth. He sat up and found something worse. He was nude and somewhere he'd never been. He reached for cover and looked around the room. His clothes were in a pile on the floor next to his shoes. There was a bucket on the bedside table with a note stuck to it.

For your puke.

He shook it and was glad to find it empty. He didn't remember puking the night before. In fact, he didn't remember much after talking to Jon-Jon in the parking lot.

Behind the bucket was a framed photo. He

picked it up to see two girls with red solo cups in their hands. One was the girl with the long blonde curly hair who was in some of his classes. She usually sat in the front, and he liked the back, mainly to keep her in his sights.

Maybe it was the Cro-Magnum man in him, but her thick hair and generous hips screamed sex. Signs of fertility men were genetically predispositioned to find attractive, right? And he did, which was why he kept his distance. He had a legacy to uphold, so girls weren't part of his big picture yet.

He looked back at the photo. Her green eyes were hidden behind thick-rimmed glasses, and her smile revealed even white teeth. The best part was he didn't think she had any idea how desirable she was. She carried herself differently from the put-together girls he hung out with. Girls who knew how to use their good looks to get what they wanted.

There was a quick knock and the door opened. Looking up, he saw the other girl from the picture. He pulled the covers closer.

"You're still here?" She put her hand on her hip.

"Yes." He cleared his throat. "Um, where is here exactly?"

"This is my place. I figured you'd call for a ride and be long gone by now."

"I will if I can find my phone." He leaned over the edge of the bed to get his pants, regretting it as dizziness overwhelmed him.

She flipped her dark hair over her shoulder and

tapped her foot. "Why aren't you wearing clothes?"

"I thought...We didn't...I mean, I am in your bed."

She shook her head. "Not my bed. My roommate. The one in the picture you're holding."

"Oh." The Y chromosome was too hard to fight sometimes. He put the frame back on the table. "I guess we hooked up."

She tilted her head to the side and raised an eyebrow before she burst out laughing. "Think again. My saintly roommate thought you might choke on your own vomit and refused to leave you alone, passed out in the parking lot." She shook her head and turned to go. "Get dressed. I'll drive you to town."

"Is your roomie here? I'd like to thank her." Really, he was too embarrassed to face her.

"No. She went to class today, unlike some people."

"Shit." He tossed back the covers and fumbled to get into his jeans. He had to turn in an assignment. Glancing at his phone to check the time, he cussed under his breath. It was almost one-thirty in the afternoon. Maybe he could catch the professor in his office.

An alarm chimed on his phone: *Meet tutor at two.*

"Dammit." He should cancel, or at least let her know he was running late.

He dashed out the bedroom door with his shirt in one hand and shoes in the other. "I've gotta go, quick."

The brunette was leaning against the kitchen

counter with a spoon of peanut butter in her hand. "Where's the fire?"

"I've missed most of the day, and I need to catch up." He jumped on one foot while he put on a shoe.

"You're wound up tight, ain't ya?"

"Not normally, but I've got a schedule. And I also think I might throw up."

She put the spoon down. "I've got something to help you with both your problems." She went to the coffee table and bent to the pumpkin.

He closed the passenger door of her pickup truck as she lit the joint, inhaled, and passed it to him. He looked at it a moment before he took it. It would calm him down, but he'd gone too far the night before; taken too much. This one last time, then he'd toss everything and get clean.

He finally learned her name was Finlee, and she dropped him at the house. He ran inside to brush his teeth and add deodorant. Extra scent covers a whole host of unrighteous smells, at least for a little while. He'd texted the tutor that he'd be a half hour late so she'd wait. In reality, it was more like forty-five minutes after he dropped by the professor's office and begged for mercy.

He ran into the library and found the room she'd reserved for them. Without first looking through the glass, he opened the door.

He was out of breath, but managed a word when he saw her. "You."

Chapter Five

Don't think about him naked. Sibba fisted her hands and pushed off the desk to stand. "You," she paused to figure out what to say, "are later than you said you'd be."

She moved around to the side of the table. "I was here at ten till two. Ten minutes early, like I am for everything." She stalked toward him. "And here you are almost an hour late."

He stood his ground and smirked. "Why didn't you wake me?"

"Because…" Her face got hot at the thought of his naked body in her bed. *Don't think about him naked.* "I'm not your keeper."

"According to Finlee, you took that responsibility on when you dragged me home with you last night."

"You ungrateful bastard. Don't think because I'm wearing hemp shoes that I won't monkey stomp you into a puddle." She leaned in and sniffed him. It

22

wasn't on his shirt, so she stood on her toes and smelled his hair. "You've been smoking weed. You better not have stolen my last joint from Jack the Jack-O-Lantern."

He laughed and put his hands up. "Wasn't me. You can talk to your roomie about sharing your things with me."

Sibba wanted to admit it wasn't technically hers anymore, but she overflowed with righteous indignation. "I can't believe you'd come to study on something. Haven't you ever heard of state-dependent learning?"

Good. She wasn't thinking about him naked. Oh, damn.

He ran his hand through his hair and sighed before he plopped down in the chair. "No, I haven't. Let the lecture commence." He leaned back and propped his feet on the table.

Instead of letting him upset her further, she let her steam run out in a long exhale as she stuffed her books into her bag. She slung it over her shoulder. "If Dr. Ferguson tries to get me in trouble or withhold my letter of recommendation, I'll tell him you use." She hated being a tattletale, but she had to cover her ass and do a better job at it than she had of covering his the night before. *Dammit.*

"Wait." He stood and reached out, touching her arm. "As long as we're both here, we should study."

She looked where his fingers gripped her lightly and didn't imagine the shiver running over her skin. *Damn pheromones.* She adjusted her glasses before she looked up into his eyes. "State-dependent learning means the state you learn in needs to be the state you test in. Or you can't recall the information. Your brain processes it differently."

"So, if I study high, I need to test high?"

"Yes."

"Does that count for other things too? Like prescription meds?"

"Yes."

He sat down hard and dropped his head into his hands. "I need help."

"Maybe we can reschedule for another time, when you're not on something."

"No, I mean I..." He lifted his head and looked at her. Weariness flashed in his eyes. "Never mind."

She waited for him to say something else, but he just watched her. The way his eyes focused on her made her shuffle her feet and want to hide. "Okay, so...we'll reschedule. Or if you're too busy, we can say we gave it the old college try."

He laughed. "You're cute."

***

Nash watched her cheeks turn pink. He stood and extended his hand. "I'm Nash, and I'm sorry I was late."

She looked at his hand a moment before she put her dainty one in his. "Sibba and don't let it happen again."

"Yes, ma'am." He tried a Southern accent.

"Don't do that. It's insulting. Like you think we're stupid because of the way we talk, and you're making fun of us."

"I like your accent. It's sexy."

Her cheeks were fully red now. "No, it's not. If

I could turn it off, I would."

"Why would you want to get rid of a part of yourself?"

"So non-Southerners, like you, don't think I'm stupid." She pulled her hand away.

"Uncle Mike's not a Southerner, and he thinks you're super-smart. His words."

Her brows knitted together. "Who? Is that Dr. Mike Ferguson?"

"Yeah. I bet you're surprised we Yankees call non-relatives aunt and uncle." He grinned.

She returned a small smile. "Where are y'all from?"

"New York."

She got a dreamy look in her eyes. "I want to go there someday."

"I guess we both want to get away from where we grew up." Chad's face flashed in his mind.

"Yeah, well, I have to get to class."

"How about tomorrow morning? Here? Is ten too early?" He was supposed to camp out with some brothers that night, but he'd drive out for a few hours and then go home to sleep. He didn't want to let her down again.

After looking at her phone, she said, "Okay. See ya then."

He almost invited her to the campsite. It would turn into a big party, and he needed her to like him. He didn't want Uncle Mike to find out about his little problem, and he couldn't let his parents down. With Chad gone, it was up to him to fulfill their dreams.

She turned to go, and he stepped closer. She

smelled like apples and cinnamon. "Let me walk you out."

She looked at him and pushed her glasses further up onto her nose. "It's okay, but thanks."

"I guess I should thank you, too."

"What for?"

His cheeks were probably the same shade at hers. "Last night."

He watched her hips as she walked away. He couldn't tell if it was a dress or a long top she wore, but she had leggings on underneath. They hugged her thighs, and he wanted to do the same.

When the door closed, blocking her from his sight, he shook himself. He couldn't think about her that way if she was going to tutor him, but it would be nice to be close to her.

He checked his watch and sat, resting his head in his hands. He had a half-hour before he had to meet the council, so he opened a textbook. His eyes grew heavy as he read. The second time his head fell off his supporting fist, he reached in his pocket for the baggie. He didn't have many left. Maybe he could take one and start weaning himself off.

Nearly tearing the bag, he shoved them back in his pocket. He needed to be able to think. He had to get control of his life again.

Chapter Six

Sibba put her finger on the page to hold her place when Finlee came in.

"Grab a warm jacket. We're going to the bonfire out at the Franklin farm." Finlee held up two coats, trying to pick between them.

Sibba groaned and tucked her fuzzy-socked feet under her. The weather had turned cold and all she wanted to do was snuggle under a blanket with a book.

"It's Friday night, and we're twenty years old, too young to stay in." Finlee threw one of the jackets on the back of the couch.

Sibba thought about lying to her bestie and saying she needed to study, but the thought of a bonfire and roasted marshmallows held some appeal. "Okay." She got up and went to the pantry.

"Ah, Sibba-dibba-doo, we're going to a keg party, not a weeny roast."

"Ooh, weenies. Great idea." Sibba opened the

refrigerator.

Finlee nearly shut her in the fridge. "No. Just no. If you want a weeny, it needs to be attached to a man. How about the godson? Did you see his weeny?"

Heat spread up her neck, and Sibba turned so her friend couldn't read her expression.

Finlee gasped. "You did. You saw it and you liked it. If you didn't, you wouldn't have a fuchsia face right now."

"I tried not to, but I couldn't help it."

"You need someone to erase the memories of what's-his-name. This could be the one."

Sibba thought about Reid, a guy she'd dated in high school until he got heavy-handed. The drama surrounding their relationship was why Jon-Jon would forever be her savior.

Finlee had been dating Jon-Jon, so Sibba was riding with them to a party. Two of Jon-Jon's friends had climbed in the back seat with her. When they'd arrived at the party, Sibba leaned over one of the guys, stuck her head out of the window, and yelled hello to Reid.

He'd pulled her out the car window by her head.

The guys were so stunned they didn't do anything to stop him, but Jon-Jon jumped out and tackled Reid. When it was over, both guys had broken noses, and she was bleeding from the cut her wire-rimmed glasses had made on her face.

She reached for the scar, remembering, and her fingers bumped her thick plastic frames. They helped conceal the evidence.

The doctor stitching her face in the emergency room that night was who made her want to pursue medicine. She could help people and make a difference in someone's life.

Sibba clutched the marshmallows to her chest as Finlee tried to pry them from her fingers. "I'm taking these or I'm not going."

"Stubborn girl." Finlee relinquished the bag. "What about this Nash fella, then?"

"I can't date the guy. I'm only going to tutor him to get my letter and stay out of jail."

***

Nash threw another log on the bonfire before he sat on one of the wooden benches they'd brought for seating. Ten tents had been set up in a circle around the fire, but there were at least seventy-five people trying to huddle closer to the flames. When word got out about an off-campus party, it drew all kinds, not just the Greek contingent.

"Ooh, Laith likey. See ya later, man." Laith slapped Nash's knee as he stood.

His seat was only vacant for half a second before Nash's ride took it. "I forgot to ask, how was it last night? You want some more?"

Nash looked at Jon-Jon without fully turning his head. "No. I'm gonna skip it. Thanks anyway."

"Didn't do it for you, huh? I'll see what else I can get, but it'll be a few days."

"No rush." Nash didn't have the courage to tell him he was going to quit. He'd do it later, when he didn't have a beer in his hand.

Jon-Jon stood and cat-called before he waved someone over. Nash decided to go mingle until he saw it was Sibba who approached.

"There's my girl." Jon-Jon hugged her. "Here, you can sit on my lap."

She smiled. "That's all right. I can stand."

Nash stood. "Take my seat."

"No. I'm fine. Sit. If my legs give out, I'll let y'all know."

"Did you come out here with the wicked witch?" Jon-Jon grinned.

"Don't call her that."

"I bet she calls me worse."

"She does, but I tell her to shut up, like I'm telling you," she said, setting her jaw.

"Defending my honor. Thanks, Sibba. You're such a sweetheart. Have you met my brother, Nash?"

She grinned and ducked her head. "Yeah, we met."

"Sibba and I are studying for the MCAT together." It sounded better than saying he was too stupid to pass and needed a tutor.

"If there's something this gal knows how to do, it's study." Jon-Jon stood. "Hey sweetie, save my seat for me. I gotta go see a guy."

Sibba hesitated for a moment before she sat next to Nash. "Have you seen any long sticks around here?"

"Maybe. Why?"

She opened her coat and pulled out a bag of marshmallows, and his smile stretched from one ear to the other. "Save my place. I'll go find some."

He foraged inside the tree line and found several long sticks after interrupting a couple making out against a tree. When he returned, Sibba was denying his seat to some drunk guy.

He slid into his spot, breaking the poor guy's heart. "You're popular."

"Yeah, drunk guys love me. I must look really good through beer goggles."

Nash laughed. "You look good through any kind of goggles."

She reached into her jacket pocket and pulled out a knife. At first, he thought she was threatening him because he'd complimented her, but she took a stick from him and started shaving one end to a point. She was pure country and he liked it. He could see why Uncle Mike had fallen for a Southern Belle and settled down south to be near her family.

He held his marshmallow over the flame next to Sibba's. "We should try this with hot dogs."

Sibba laughed. "I tried to bring some, but Finlee wouldn't let me."

"We should go to the store and get some after we finish our flaming sugar on a stick." He blew on his and then put it in his mouth. It melted on his tongue, and he closed his eyes, savoring the flavor.

"Good, huh?"

He opened his eyes to see Sibba smiling with white goo on her lips. Before he could stop himself, he leaned in and kissed her.

Chapter Seven

Blue lights flashed in the rearview mirror, and for the second time in one night, Sibba thought she might have a heart attack. By the time her warm gooey kiss with Nash had ended, with cheering from the people close by, it felt as though a spark from the fire had landed on her and spread across her skin. She thought the fire department might have to come put her out. It was that kind of kiss. Hot.

"Tell me again why we agreed to make a midnight marshmallow run." She looked for a place to pull over.

"At least we got rid of Eddie already. He was wasted...and into you."

Eddie was the boy who'd hit on her and insulted her the night before. He'd bummed a ride to town with them.

"He was into me because he was wasted." She looked at Nash as she put it in park, her face serious. "You got anything on you?"

He patted his pockets with wide eyes. "No."

She took a few deep breaths to settle her racing heart while she dug through her purse for her wallet. With a glance in the mirror, she saw two officers with flashlights going around both sides of her car. She lowered the window and let the chilly wind cool her hot face.

"License and registration." The officer shined his flashlight in her eyes, causing her to wince and turn her head.

She handed him the requested information. "What's the problem, officer?"

"Did you know you have a tail light out?"

"No, I didn't. It must've happened recently because my dad checks my car every Sunday when I go home."

He examined the license. "Home to Beulah, huh? You any relation to Chief Douglas?"

"Yes, sir, he's my dad."

The other officer, who'd been interviewing Nash leaned down. "What do you think your dad would say about that open container in your back seat?"

Sibba twisted around to see what the officer was talking about. There was a beer bottle buckled into the seatbelt in the back. She'd wondered what Eddie was doing back there clicking the belts. She should've checked after he got out.

"It's not ours," Nash explained to the police about their hitchhiker. "He must've snuck it in the car because I never saw it."

"Me either." She backed him up.

"Would you two please step out of the car?"

Sibba closed her eyes and nodded her head as she reached for the handle. "Please don't call my dad."

"We're going to search your car. Is there anything you two want to tell us about before we start?"

Nash looked at her with raised eyebrows, and she shook her head.

"Put your hands on the car." The other officer patted Nash down.

Sibba automatically faced the car and did the same. At least pressing down on the hood made her hands stop shaking.

Nash slid his hand over and covered one of hers. "Your hands are freezing."

"What do we have here?"

Oh, God. Her heart squeezed as she shivered. She racked her brain wondering if anything had been dropped under the seat. She was diligent about her car since her dad did his weekly inspection. He claimed to check the tires and oil, but she'd seen him moving floor mats and checking around inside.

The officer placed a plastic lock box on the hood in front of her.

It was worse. She'd forgotten to disclose that. "I have a concealed carry permit. That's my pistol."

"You should've told us before we searched."

"By law, I don't have to tell you, but I would have as a courtesy had I remembered it. That case lives under my seat, and I rarely touch it."

Nash squeezed her hand and tried to tell her something with his eyes.

***

Nash held onto Sibba's hand and sent her mental signals to tone it down a notch. If she gave the cops attitude, they might wind up in jail and that wouldn't help either of them get into med school.

The officer with her gun case paused to listen to something on his radio. Nash couldn't make out anything but static, a couple of numbers, and squealing before the officer pressed the button and said they were en route.

He handed the case and paperwork to Sibba. "You kids get home and stay out of trouble."

Nash moved to stand beside her as they watched the officers make a U-turn, blaring the siren as they sped away.

Sibba's hand landed on her chest. "Oh, my God. I thought I was in big trouble."

Nash put his arm around her. "Thank goodness for the 11-79, whatever that is."

"It's fortunate for us, but not for whoever was in the car accident where they're sending an ambulance."

He squeezed her shoulder. "I hope they're all right."

She leaned into him a little. "Me too."

"Are you still up for roasting food on sticks over a fire?"

She smiled. "Yeah, but I reckon I need to get a tail light while we're at Wally World."

"I'll put it in for you."

She furrowed her brows and turned to him. "You know how to do that?"

"Just 'cause I'm from the big city, doesn't

mean I can't take care of business."

She put a hand on her generous hip and tilted her head.

"My mom's brother owns an auto repair shop in upstate New York. My brother and I used to spend summers there."

Nash hadn't thought about it in years. Chad hadn't been a fan of the grease, saying he needed to keep his hands clean so he could be a surgeon someday. Nash thought more dirt and grease proved he was doing something important. After Chad died, Nash realized his brother's dream had been important. So much so, he needed to keep it alive, despite his ineptitude for biology.

The wind blew and he caught a whiff of cinnamon from Sibba. He hugged her closer. "You smell so good."

"Ah, thanks. We should probably go." She pulled her warmth away from him, leaving cold empty air in her place.

He shook it off. He'd never had a problem letting go of a girl before, but something about Sibba felt right.

Before they left to go back to the party, Nash changed the tail light in the parking lot. Sibba watched with her arms wrapped around herself.

"I hope the bonfire's still going strong. Get in the car before you freeze. I'm almost done." He fitted the red plastic cover into its slots and pressed it into place.

She reached in and turned the lights on before walking around to check they were working. "I'm impressed."

"Didn't trust me to get it right, did you?" He winked. "I'm good at a few things."

"Yeah, like kissing. We can't do that again."

"As soon as you quit looking and smelling so good, I'll stop."

She shook her head and shoved him lightly, causing him to drop the empty paper and plastic wrapper the light came in.

The wind picked it up and carried it in the air. Sibba laughed and chased after it, but each time she got close, it blew further away. Her laugh was contagious, and he also ran after the flying debris, jumping to catch it at the same time she did. They bumped into each other, and he closed his arms around her again.

"Got it." She stepped out of his embrace.

He bent to rest his elbows on his thighs and catch his breath. "It's a good thing those cops weren't here to witness that. They'd think we're on something for sure."

"High on life." She doubled over with laughter again.

Turning away, he pulled at his collar. He wasn't clean yet, but he didn't want her to know, sensing the knowledge wouldn't make her happy. In his defense, the pills he took were prescription.

They just weren't prescribed to him.

Chapter Eight

Sibba bumped Nash's arm with her elbow as she spread the books and study guides out on the dining table. They'd relocated when they'd found the library closed. The only bad thing about having Nash in her kitchen was her bedroom was steps away down the hall, and he'd been naked in her bed. She wished she could get the image out of her head because then she'd be able to put her foot down and stop the touchy-friendly way he treated her.

Who was she kidding? She liked it when he flirted with her and would even if she hadn't seen him in the buff. The problem was she couldn't see any good coming of it. She needed her letter from Dr. F. That was the only reason they were together. It helped that Nash wasn't the spoiled rich boy she'd imagined him to be.

"I had to drive a bunch of drunk people home in a borrowed vehicle last night." He shifted in his seat and put a hand on the back of her chair.

She'd left around two, and he'd walked her to her car.

"That's what I get for being drunk on sugar instead of beer." He grinned. "Plus, my ride left me. Remind me to never go anywhere with Jon-Jon again."

She smiled. "I don't know. He usually looks out for his peeps."

"That's true, which makes it stranger that he left me. I texted and called, but never heard back from him." He propped his elbow on the table. "He seems to have a thing for you."

"What?" She scrunched her face. "No. He's my hero from way back, so he thinks it's his duty to look out for me."

"Hero, huh?" His eyes studied her face and landed on her cheekbone.

He turned in his seat and maneuvered her chair to face him. The sound of wooden legs scraping against tile echoed through the room. She fidgeted.

Without asking, he removed her glasses. He shifted back in his seat to study her face before he leaned in and cupped her cheek.

Sure he was about to kiss her again, she started to pull away, but he lifted his hand and turned it so the backs of his fingers grazed her cheekbone.

"Your eyes are beautiful."

Her mouth was dry, so she forced a swallow. "Thanks."

"How did you get this?"

"The hazards of having four eyes." His grin made her head fuzzy for a second. "It's weird for

39

you to have noticed when we were talking about Jon-Jon. There was a fight at a party in high school, and I got caught in the crossfire. Jon-Jon rescued me."

The front door opened, and Finlee came in. "It's colder than a well digger's ass at the North Pole."

A cute Hispanic guy came in the door after her.

"Laith?" Nash looked confused before he made introductions.

Laith held up a bag from Hardees. "We stopped for biscuits and got extra."

"Coffee." Finlee's teeth chattered.

"Why are you so cold?" Sibba stood to get mugs. "Did you sleep outside?"

"Yes." She blew on her fingers.

Laith put his arm around her. "She shared my tent."

Sibba stopped herself from rolling her eyes by looking at her phone. She hit ignore when she saw it was her dad calling. It wasn't like Finlee hadn't ever slept outside, or hadn't ever slept with a hot guy she barely knew. It was the small world feeling of it. And, when something went wrong, Sibba wouldn't be able to have Nash over again because best friend solidarity dictated friends didn't remain friendly with exes or their friends.

Jon-Jon had been a special exception, and Sibba was still inclined to believe he was technically right, even if he was morally repugnant. Finlee had gotten mad at him at a party one night and broken up with him. When she stopped by his house to make up the next morning, he'd hooked up with another girl. If Jon-Jon hadn't saved Sibba and formed a special bond with her, Finlee wouldn't have tolerated their friendship.

Finlee's phone rang and she pulled it from her pocket to look at the display. "Why is your dad calling me?"

Sibba reached for the phone as an uneasy feeling crept into her chest.

***

Nash put a hand on Sibba's shoulder when he noticed the first tear. She shook as her face fell in her hand.

Finlee shoved a paper towel toward her. "What's wrong, Sib?"

Sibba put up a finger to silence her while she nodded at the voice on the phone. "You're sure?" She sucked in a shaky breath. "What can I do?"

She handed the phone back to Finlee. "It's Jon-Jon." A strangled sound came from her throat. "He was killed in a car accident last night."

An invisible blow landed in the center of Nash's chest, knocking the wind out of him. His mouth hung open, and he blinked a few times to be sure he'd heard correctly.

Laith sat down hard in the chair next to him.

Finlee paced and called out to God.

Sibba turned to Nash with tears welling in her eyes. "That wreck we passed last night on the way back to the party…" Her breath hitched. "He wrapped his car around a tree. Dead on the scene."

A loud ringing filled his ears, taking him back several years to when he couldn't save his real brother.

Now, another brother was dead, and Nash asked himself the same old questions. *What could I have done differently? How could I have prevented it? Why didn't I have the courage to make a stand?*

If he'd been honest with Jon-Jon about cleaning up his act the night before, it might have made a difference.

With one arm around Sibba, who was crying on his shoulder, he ran his free hand through his hair. "This is my fault."

All eyes turned to him.

"How?" Laith asked.

"If I'd been there to drive him or at least stop him from driving…"

"As if he'd let you drive his baby." Sibba put her glasses back on.

"Or let anyone stop him from doing what he wanted to do." Finlee gripped the back of a chair.

"If you'd been with him, you might be dead too." Laith rubbed his eyes. "And he was always on something. Drove like that all the time."

"I know, but if I hadn't left with Sibba…" He stopped, not wanting Sibba to think it was her fault.

Chapter Nine

Sunday afternoon, Sibba sat in the front passenger seat of Nash's Lexus as he drove them to Jon-Jon's parents' house. Finlee and Laith rode in the back. When Sibba had called ahead to make sure they'd be home, her own mother had answered the phone. She'd arrived after church with food for the family and then stayed to help organize the kitchen and field phone calls.

When they arrived, Sibba hugged and cried with Miss Vera and let Finlee do the same before she introduced Nash and Laith as Jon-Jon's fraternity brothers. Then, she left them to go to the kitchen.

Her mama held her for a long time. "His brothers have been calling. A big group of them are planning to come one night this week."

"We've got mid-terms. This is gonna be hard."

"Life is so short, baby. We know that better than anyone, don't we?" Her mama brushed Sibba's

43

hair over her shoulder.

Sibba nodded as tears fell. Her mama amazed her. She wasn't sure she would be as strong under the circumstances.

That night, her books were spread in front of her on the dining table as she tried to concentrate on her studies. She kept glancing up at Nash, who'd needed some time away from the house where the brothers were mourning.

He sighed and pushed away from the table. "This just brings up memories of my own brother, you know?"

She blinked at him. "No, I don't. What happened to your brother?"

Nash scratched his jaw and looked away, like he was looking through time to the past. "A girl fell through the ice, and Chad rushed to help. I was scared to venture too close to the hole for fear we'd all go in. Chad pulled the girl out, and I gave her my coat and led her to more solid ground. We were a few steps away when I heard the cracking noise."

Sadness wrinkled the corner of his eyes and Sibba's heart bled for him.

"That sound still haunts my dreams some nights. I wake up in a cold sweat every time."

Sibba angled her body to face him, and she leaned closer, taking one of his hands in both of hers.

"I turned in time to see the splash after the ice gave way. I crawled to the edge and reached for him. I had his hand in my grip, and I pulled with all my strength." Nash shook his head. "Chad was two years older and only ten pounds heavier than me, but in those wet winter clothes, he felt like a thousand pounds."

Sibba swallowed around the lump in her throat and rubbed his arm.

"I waited for that surge of adrenaline you hear about, the one that helps moms lift cars off their kids." He put his hand over his eyes. "It never came. At least not in time to save Chad before the ice began to crack more. He let go. He saw the panic in my eyes, and he let go of my hand and sank under the surface."

Nash's muscles bunched under Sibba's grip.

"I screamed and scooted around on my hands and knees, trying to see beneath the ice, trying to find a way to save him. I failed. Chad's dead because I couldn't find the strength or the way out."

Sibba blinked and tears streamed down her face. "Oh, Nash." She wrapped her arms around him while he sat, his shoulders slumped forward in defeat.

The worst part was the hurt he still carried and how he was still trying to make it right. She pulled back to wipe her already raw eyes. "Is that why you want to be a doctor? So you can save people?"

He shrugged. "It's what I told my parents I wanted to do after Chad's funeral. They jumped on the idea, and I never had a chance to consider anything else, even when I struggled through high school science. I guess I'm just dumb that way."

"Or stubborn." She grinned a watery smile. "Determination can get you a long way. I'm not naturally smart like everyone thinks. I pick things up quickly, but unless I cement it in my brain, I forget."

"What made you so determined?"

"Being told I couldn't." She let out a long breath. "I was a twin. We were born prematurely and weighed under four pounds each. Preemies have a lot of developmental problems." She touched one arm of her glasses. "That's why I have these."

"Can you not wear contacts?"

"Don't want to." She touched her scar.

He reached out and took her fingers in his. "It doesn't detract from your beauty."

That must be something Northern boys learn to say because Southern ones never said things like that. Especially not to her. She'd never had a boy look at her the way Nash did either. It caused her skin to heat and her heart to beat faster.

"What happened to your twin?"

She'd forgotten what she'd been saying while his brown eyes bore into her soul. "Well, that's the strange thing. He was bigger and stronger than me. They worried I wouldn't make it, but when we were eleven months old, he died of SIDS."

"Your poor parents."

"I know. I feel sorry for myself sometimes, but my parents are the ones who suffered. Needless to say, they became overprotective of me."

"Which is why you can't wait to leave here."

She shrugged as the old familiar weight settled on her shoulders.

"You have survivor's guilt like I do." He squeezed her hand. "I'm surprised at your mom being there for Jon-Jon's family. I imagine it's tough."

"Mama started a support group for parents who've lost children. It's her ministry."

"I wish my parents had something like that. Instead, they put all their hopes in me, and I'm so afraid I'll let them down."

"I know the feeling. The determination thing. That came when I started school. My parents met with the teacher and principal and I overheard. They were going to put me in Special Ed because of my learning difficulties. They told my parents not to expect too much from me academically. I was only five, but I set out to prove them wrong. When I gave my valedictorian speech at commencement, I thanked them for lighting a fire under my ass."

***

Nash laughed. "Please, tell me you said it just like that."

"I wanted to, but I didn't want to shame my parents, so I used a little tact."

God, he'd known her three days and was falling for her already. He'd never met anyone like Sibba Douglas. She was direct and determined, yet tolerant and understanding. Opening up to her, which was something he hadn't done with anyone, helped him feel like his burden was a little lighter.

"Can I come over and study this week?"

"Yeah. I can see why you'd need a break from the house. Thanks for sharing your story with me." She squeezed his arm again. "I know it's not easy, but don't forget to mourn Jon-Jon. He was your friend...and brother too, I guess. Sorry, I don't get that part as much. I suppose it'd be like me having a bunch of Finlees. She's like a sister to me."

"I'm not sure the world can handle a bunch of Finlees." He grinned and picked up a strand of her hair. "You knew Jon-Jon a lot longer than I did. Tell me about a fun time you guys had."

"He made me go to prom when he was dating Finlee. I still had stitches." She pointed to her eye. "My boyfriend and I had just broken up, and Jon-Jon said he'd be the lucky guy with two dates. He was always so sweet to me." She dabbed at the corner of her eye with a tissue.

"I told you I thought he had a thing for you."

She smiled and shook her head. "He treated me like a kid sister. I guess I treated him like the brother I missed out on. Anyway, dress up dances are not my thing. I have no coordination and the outfits girls have to wear to those things aren't my style."

"Formal wear?"

"Yeah, Finlee bought two similar dresses and let me borrow one. Actually, she bought the one I wore for me, but pretended she couldn't decide."

"What did it look like?"

"It was tie-dyed."

"No way." He couldn't fight a grin.

"Yes way. Wanna see a picture?"

He nodded. "I won't believe it otherwise."

She went into her room and came back with a five-by-seven photo. Jon-Jon was in the center, flanked by Sibba on one side and Finlee on the other.

Nash's heart hurt as his finger grazed over his friend's face. Jon-Jon wore a huge smile, extremely proud to have two pretty girls to escort. His tie and cummerbund were pink to match Finlee's dress, but they also matched the pink streaks in Sibba's. The scarred side of her face was away from the camera. She wasn't wearing glasses in the picture, but she pointed out the edge of a metal frame sticking out of Jon-Jon's coat pocket.

He looked from the image to the real thing. "You shouldn't be ashamed, you know. It wasn't your fault."

"It's a constant reminder of how stupid I was."

He cupped her cheek. "You are not stupid."

"Neither are you." She tapped the study guide. "We need to focus."

Nash had trouble concentrating with her cinnamon scent invading his lungs.

Chapter Ten

Sibba didn't own a black dress. The Saturday morning of the funeral she went shopping to find something respectful enough to say goodbye in and still reflect her style. Jon-Jon would appreciate it if he knew.

The weather had warmed again, but she'd still need a layer under the sheer crinkle dress she'd picked out. She had the perfect silver belt with buckles all around to cinch her waist. Thinking about clothes was a good distraction to keep her from thinking about her friend being gone too soon and how he'd never be stopping by again to see her. Pressure built behind her eyes and her heart ached.

She'd been to visit Jon-Jon's parents three times: the first with Finlee, Nash, and Laith; the second with her parents; and the third with Nash again. They'd asked him to be a pallbearer.

She and Nash had seen each other every day during the week under the pretense of studying. The time was spent talking and sharing their hurts. He told her about his substance abuse. Sibba wasn't surprised. More than half the people she knew at school used, and Jon-Jon had been one of them. Her dad was privy to the autopsy report and had told her about all the drugs in his system. His liver also had signs of damage from the abuse.

She pressed her fingertips against her forehead. So much crying had given her a perpetual headache, but she refused to take even an aspirin. She wanted her system clean. She'd even begun researching holistic medicine.

She paid for her purchases and went home where Finlee was getting ready and beating herself up for not having been nicer to Jon-Jon. It seemed like all of them wanted to accept some of the blame and redirect the horror of losing someone so young.

The college had brought in grief counselors since Jon-Jon had so many friends. The little church in Beulah was expected to be packed. Her dad would be helping with traffic, and students were encouraged to carpool, which was one of the reasons Nash and Laith were picking up Sibba and Finlee.

Sibba was trying to tame her curls when they knocked. Finlee let them in, and Nash came to her open bathroom door. They'd stopped asking each other how they were doing. It was a dumb question considering they were all grieving.

He stepped in, put his hand on her back, and kissed her cheek. "You look beautiful."

She glanced down and smiled. It always made her uncomfortable when people said that. She didn't feel beautiful, so hearing it always made her question if they were telling the truth.

"Thanks." She made herself look at him. "You clean up nice."

She wished she could give a direct compliment without feeling embarrassed. He looked better than nice. His black suit looked tailor made, and his white shirt was open at the neck.

He held up a tie. "Can you help me with this?"

She smiled, thankful she'd spent hours of her childhood playing with her dad's ties. He only wore them to church on Sundays, but he'd taught her how to make a Windsor knot.

She put the tie around her own neck to get it started, and then transferred it to Nash's. His eyes never left her face, and she put all her concentration on the thin piece of material. He was too intense for her, making her feel things she shouldn't feel. Want things she shouldn't want.

***

Nash inhaled apples and cinnamon as Sibba straightened his tie.

She patted his chest. "There. Handsome as ever." And then she blushed.

He grinned. He'd begun to think she didn't find him attractive since she'd dodged his efforts to kiss her. While he had her confined in the small bathroom, he decided to take another chance.

He looked her square in the eyes and lowered his head slowly, giving her every opportunity to turn away. She didn't and when he captured her lips with his, he circled his arms around her, drawing her against his chest. With one hand, he stroked her back while his other tangled in her thick hair. He coaxed her lips apart, and she let him in. A soft moan from her elicited the same feeling in his chest as a shot of Fireball whisky left in the mouth—a good burn. He got lost in her, and it was exactly where he wanted to be.

Unsure how long they'd been lip-locked, it took some throat-clearing and taunting to intrude into his thoughts.

"Air break, people." Finlee's voice was unwelcome.

He broke the kiss and looked at Sibba from beneath heavy lids. Her eyes were closed and her mouth was open. Glad she seemed dazed, he gave her a quick peck before he turned to their audience.

Laith's grin spoke volumes. "We need to get on the road, Hot-lips Lincoln."

"We're ready." Sibba blasted her hair with some spray and breezed past him.

He needed a moment to settle the throbbing in his chest and in his pants. It was probably really wrong to be horny on the way to a funeral. The kiss to end all kisses would give him something to think about if things got too deep.

It wasn't that he didn't want to mourn; he'd been grief-stricken all week. It was the expectations for men. Be strong. Don't cry. Don't be vulnerable. Don't be weak. All of his brothers would be there and since he was a casket bearer, he'd be in front where everyone could see if he lost it. He hadn't cried since his brother's funeral. He couldn't think too hard about Jon-Jon, and he definitely couldn't think about Chad. Sibba's lips would be a good distraction.

In the backseat of Laith's car, Sibba gave him a handkerchief.

He turned it over in his hands. "Hopefully, I won't need this."

"If you do, it's nothing to be ashamed of. There'll be lots of tears shed today." She squeezed his hand. "I put essential oils on it."

He lifted the white cloth to his nose and breathed in. It smelled like his Sibba, cinnamon spice and everything nice.

Fighting the pressure building behind his eyes, he kissed her cheek. "Thank you."

The hanky turned out to be his saving grace. Several times during the service when things got heavy, he lifted it to his nose and was transported into the sweet embrace of his cinnamon girl.

The family had asked the fraternity brothers if any of them wanted to speak at the service. None of them did, but they'd elected Nash to be the spokesman for the group. Normally, the president would do it, but Dave had been Jon-Jon's roommate and was too broken up.

The night before, Laith and a few others helped Nash write down some ideas, and they were on an index card in his coat pocket. He hadn't told Sibba he was doing it, which was one of the reasons he was surprised when the pastor called her to the podium.

Chapter Eleven

Sibba wiped her sweaty hands on her black cotton and lace handkerchief. It didn't help much since it was already damp from the tears she'd shed. Her glasses were smudged from being removed, replaced, and repositioned so often. She took a tissue from a box she passed on the way to the altar. Trying to clean her lenses only made them worse. It was just as well. This way she couldn't see the eyes watching her. She had no notes to read because Jon-Jon's parents asked her to speak from the heart.

She looked in their direction and swallowed before she spoke. "When Mr. John and Miss Vera asked me to say a few words, I didn't think I'd be able to, but they want to celebrate Jon-Jon's life. Everyone who knew him, knows he could've written the book on celebrating. It all began at the famous Andrews' pool party when he decided skinny-dipping would liven things up."

The crowd laughed.

"He was only six years old then, but it caused quite a stir, and it was the beginning of a trend. Jon-Jon will go down in Beulah history as the only person to successfully evade the law while streaking down Main Street during the Cotton Festival parade. Thanks to Mr. John for putting a stop to that particular behavior. I can't imagine what college would've been like if he'd kept it up."

"It was your dad that stopped it." Mr. John grinned.

More laughter.

"Great. Thanks, Dad." Her dad wasn't inside the church to hear, but she said it anyway.

"Jon-Jon loved life, and he loved to have a good time. While most of us dream of living and the things we'll do one day, he lived in every moment. He wasn't perfect, but then none of us are, and if he got another chance, I really don't think he'd change a thing. Besides knowing how to have fun, he had a big heart. He never met a stranger, and he made even the most awkward among us feel included." She waved her hand in the air when she said the last line to indicate she was speaking about herself.

She glanced behind the family to where many people they'd grown up with were seated and a few of them chuckled and raised their hands too.

Her eyes filled with tears again, and she dabbed at her cheeks while waiting for the lump in her throat to dissolve. "In high school, Jon-Jon was famous for quoting Horace. *Carpe diem, quam minimum credula postero*, which translates as 'seize the day, trusting as little as possible in the next day.' He knew tomorrow wasn't promised to any of us, so the best way to honor his memory is to live every moment like it might be our last."

She paused to inhale, and the exhale was a little shaky. "Jon-Jon," she looked heavenward, "thank you for making our days a little brighter."

"Carpe diem." A chorus of voices from the Beulah High School section filled the air.

It made her laugh and cry at the same time. She made her way past her pew and out into the alcove, where she took a few breaths. The exterior door was right in front of her, and she was debating stepping out for fresh air when an arm slid around her shoulders.

A deep voice she hadn't heard in years spoke in her ear. "Nice speech."

She stiffened, and he squeezed her arm. "Don't be scared. Let's step outside."

Her feet moved even though a little voice in the back of her brain was yelling for her to go back in. Once outside, she tried to extricate herself from his grip, but he turned to face her and held both her arms.

"Don't be afraid of me, Sibba."

She made herself look up at Reid. He was a blur because of her glasses, so she reached up to remove them and turned her scarred side toward him. "I have every reason to be. What are you doing here?"

"I'm here to apologize. I never got to make peace with Jon-Jon, and now it's too late. Let me make peace with you."

Sibba wished someone would rescue her like Jon-Jon had. She was upset enough without adding

Reid and their history to the mix.

She took a deep breath. "You already apologized that day in court, remember? That's why the judge let you off with a slap on the wrist."

"I know what I did was wrong, and that you'll never trust me, but I'm truly sorry I hurt you. I was coked out that night, and I guess my jealousy needed an outlet. Seeing you with those other guys made me snap. I'm glad Jon-Jon was there to stop me."

She examined the bump in his nasal bone and was glad once again Jon-Jon had gotten that lick in. Though rumor had it she did it when her elbow hit Reid's face. It was the only flaw on an otherwise perfect face. She didn't want to forgive, didn't want to be civil, but she was too full of hurt at the moment to deal with him.

She wiped the lenses of her glasses and replaced them. "All right."

"All right what?" He tilted his head and grinned.

"I accept your apology."

"Do you think his parents will talk to me?"

"It's probably best not to do it here. Maybe call or visit them at home later."

Her body tensed as he hugged her. "You were always so smart. I knew you'd have good advice."

"Get your damn hands off my daughter."

Sibba looked up to see her dad stalking toward them, one hand on his sidearm and anger in his eyes.

Reid let go of her and took a step back.

"Dad, please, not so loud." She nodded toward

the church.

"Get the hell away from her." It was scarier when his voice came out like a low growl.

"He was just trying to apologize. Let it go, please." Fearing a churchyard brawl, she bunched her skirt in her fists.

"I can't let go of the fact that your face will never be the same, and I can't let him come in here and disrupt this service."

"He's not."

Reid put his hands up. "I'm not. I'm leaving." He backed away. "Sibba, I am sorry." He put his hand over his heart before he turned.

"He didn't hurt you did he, baby?" Her dad put his hands on her face and arms to examine her. "Lying sack of no good, piece of shit-pie…" His words turned to mumbling.

"Sibba."

She turned to see Nash on the steps of the church, watching her dad check her over.

He came closer. "Is everything okay?"

"Yeah, this is my dad. Dad, this is Nash."

Her dad turned to him. "You're not trying to date my daughter, are you?"

Nash's eyes widened. "No, we're friends and study buddies. I don't date, so I can focus on academics."

Sibba deflated as she wondered what he'd been doing putting the moves on her if he didn't plan on dating her. She tried to reason it out in her head, but she just wound up mad at herself for being so naive.

"I'm going back in." Sibba didn't look at either of them as she strode up the stairs and back into the church.

***

Nash stood next to Sibba's father and watched her go. He started to follow until the man stopped him with a hand on his arm.

"Tell me about your people." He crossed his arms over his chest.

Nash gave him the run down: hometown, parent's occupations, college major, and future plans.

"Why do you want to be a doctor?"

He had a canned answer, the noble one, which got nods of approval each time he gave it. But, it felt fake. Something about Sibba's father in his police uniform compelled him be honest.

"My brother wanted to be a doctor. When he died, my parents thought my pursuing his dream would be a good way to honor him, so that's what I'm trying to do."

"Have you done your intern hours?"

"Not yet. Sibba did hers with my godfather, and I'll do them there too, but I've been procrastinating because," he took a deep breath, "I'm not good with blood."

Mr. Douglas laughed. "Then you might be going into the wrong field."

Nash sighed and shoved his hands in his pockets. "I know. I think Sibba knows it too, but she's too nice to say so."

"If you could pick, do anything you wanted, what would you do?"

Nash thought about it. There were tons of things he wanted to try to see if he had an aptitude for them, like flying a plane or something finance related. He was good at math. Whatever he did, it needed to pay well so he could support a family someday. Sibba flashed in his mind and he pulled the handkerchief from his pocket and wiped his brow, smelling the soothing scent at the same time.

A thought he'd never had hit him.

He and Sibba had spent a lot of time talking about death. They'd both spoken to grief counselors. Sharing his thoughts with someone made him feel less alone in his struggle. It even helped him put some of the past to rest where his brother was concerned.

"I think…I'm not sure, but maybe counseling?" He wondered if his college credits would apply toward that degree.

"That's kind of related to what you've been working on." Mr. Douglas uncrossed his arms and put his hands on his hips. "I hear clinical psychologists do well and a lot of them go to work for the Feds, profiling and what not."

"I need to look into it more, but thanks for talking it out with me." Looking up at the clear, blue sky, a new hope filled him.

"No problem. Listen, I need to ask a favor."

Nash swallowed, unsure what he was getting into.

Her dad sidled closer and lowered his voice. "When Sibba graduated high school, Jon-Jon came to me and told me he'd look out for her if she went to his college. I made sure she did, even though she pitched a fit. She has my adventurous spirit, and she can't wait to get the hell out of Dodge."

"Once she's been out in the world, she probably won't think home is so bad."

"I just want her to be happy…and safe, which is where you come in. I'd like you to keep an eye on her. If you see her at parties and such, make sure she's not getting hassled by drunk boys who can't appreciate a good thing when they see it."

Nash smiled inside, but didn't let it show on his face. He could appreciate Sibba and did, very much. "It would be my pleasure to look out for her." He took a deep breath. "I'd like to ask your permission to take her to Winter Formal."

"What's that, like the prom?"

"Sort of, it's a banquet to honor our Senior fraternity brothers. There's a dinner and dancing."

"I don't have a problem with her going with you, but she's not big on formal events. Finlee and Jon-Jon had to drag her to the prom."

"Did she not get asked?" Nash didn't want to let on he knew a little about it.

"Oh, she got asked. A few boys even came straight to me like you're doing, but I never told her. Her boyfriend attacked her a few weeks before, and she never had any interest in dating after that."

"That scar on her cheek, is it from the attack?"

Mr. Douglas nodded, and Nash clenched his fists as a righteous fury rose up in him. Sibba had omitted some major details.

Mr. Douglas slapped him on the back. "I feel the same way, son. I wanted to wring his damn neck when I saw his hands on her a few minutes ago."

"That was him?" Nash's voice pitched high on the last word.

"Yeah, he hasn't been back here since he graduated high school. Just seeing him makes my blood boil." A muscle in his jaw ticked.

"Maybe he'll crawl back to whatever rock he was hiding under, but I'll be more diligent now that I know he's around."

"You own a gun?"

"No, but maybe you can help me."

Chapter Twelve

Sibba looked over her shoulder toward the back of the church for the tenth time. The service was nearly over, and Nash hadn't returned. She hoped her dad wasn't threatening him.

As the last song played, she saw him weave through the crowd on the side wall of the church and return to his spot in the front pew across the aisle from the family. She was sorry she'd missed his speech, but she hadn't known he'd planned to speak.

Sibba got ready to go out with Finlee and their classmates, knowing Nash would be one of the first to leave, carrying the casket.

The cemetery was right next to the church, so they walked toward the tent, which had been erected over the grave site. The family filled the rows of chairs under the covering, and the pallbearers stood in a line on the other side of the grave. The rest of the people crowded around for the interment.

When the final "Amen" was said, Sibba and Finlee got in the receiving line. She intended to save a place for Nash because that's what friends and study buddies did for each other. She decided not to be upset. She'd let herself get sucked into a little fantasy about having a nice boyfriend who shared her goal of getting into medical school.

When she spotted him in a throng of fraternity boys, he was hugging a tall, blonde girl. Her black dress fit her like a hot dog casing that had boiled too long. Something might bust loose. If it did, the guys would be thrilled because it would burst in all the right places. The worst part was her perfectly straight-as-an-ironing-board hair. Sibba wanted to slap her.

Touching her own unruly locks, she turned away. When she thought about her run-in with Reid, she changed her attitude. Jealousy was never pretty, and their history would forever remind her of that.

She told Finlee about the encounter in the churchyard with Reid, and her best friend was appropriately flummoxed. She could count on Finlee to threaten Reid's manhood and make good on the threat if given the chance.

Sibba placed her hand on her chest, thankful for good friends. Then, taking a deep breath, she approached Miss Vera for a hug.

"Thank you for speaking. Jon-Jon would've been tickled, and it meant so much to John and me."

Mr. John hugged her. "Come to the house and eat with us. Jon-Jon kept a picture of him and you on his mirror in his bedroom. It was a candid from that dance y'all went to."

Miss Vera squeezed her hand. "We'd like you to have it."

"I'd love to." Sibba was sure it was from the prom. Finlee had gotten a picture of them slow dancing. It was Sibba's only dance that night, and she'd stepped on Jon-Jon's feet several times. "I'll keep y'all in my prayers."

She moved away and looked around for Nash while she waited for Finlee. He still had his arms around the blonde girl, but they'd moved away from the crowd. He looked in Sibba's direction, but she swiveled her head toward another friend who wanted her attention.

"Hey." Finlee took her arm. "Let's go to Jon-Jon's parents' house for a little while."

"Sounds good to me." Sibba glanced over at Nash. "The guys are having a ceremony at their house tonight. My dad can take us home later. Will you go tell them we have another ride?"

Sibba waited for her, and when Finlee returned, they got in the back of her dad's work SUV for the short trip to the Andrews' place.

When they arrived, Finlee pulled her to the side. "I don't want you to be surprised, so I need to warn you about something."

Sibba raised her eyebrows. After seeing Reid at the funeral, she wasn't sure anything else could shock her.

"The girl at the graveside, the one with Nash, she's his…friend with benefits."

***

Nash was disappointed Sibba didn't say

goodbye before she left. He'd looked for her until he saw her leave. Then Laith had ushered him into the car. To his chagrin, Lexi climbed in the back seat. They'd had an arrangement since freshman year—sex with no strings and dates for formals, if needed.

Lexi had called it off when she started dating a guy from another fraternity at the beginning of the semester, but they'd recently broken up. Nash tried to turn her away, but she was distraught over Jon-Jon's death and needed a shoulder to cry on.

He called Sibba twice, but it went straight to voicemail. She probably still had her phone turned off from the service. He didn't like being out of touch with her. He'd come to rely on her too much in the short time they'd known each other, and that couldn't be good.

When they got to the house, the kegs had already been delivered. The guys had agreed they'd drink to Jon-Jon's memory because it was what he would've wanted, but none of them would drive. All car keys were going into a pot in the kitchen. Anyone who showed up would have to relinquish their keys.

It was rumored the cops were setting up DUI checkpoints around town, and with the accident so fresh, no one wanted to risk their lives behind the wheel. Nash only hoped it would last. He'd been guilty of driving under the influence, but thankfully, no one had gotten hurt.

The brothers took turns raising their glasses and sharing stories about Jon-Jon. Nash thought about the words he'd shared at the funeral, and he tried not to be disheartened because Sibba hadn't been there to hear them. In her defense, she hadn't known, but hearing she'd been outside with her ex who'd used her for a punching bag was upsetting. Surely she didn't still care about him. Her dad didn't think there was any chance of that. He'd invited Nash to come back to Beulah the next day, so he could teach him how to shoot. If things went well, he might enter the sporting clay contest after all.

Nash checked his phone, hoping for a message from Sibba. When the make-shift memorial service was winding down and he'd drank more than he'd intended, he went onto the veranda to call her. As soon as she answered, someone snatched his phone away from him.

"Hello, big boy."

He hated when Lexi called him that. He turned and reached for his phone, but she'd already pressed the end button.

"You don't need to call your super-smart tutor right now. You don't need a tutor when it comes to meeting my needs in the bedroom."

He looked over her shoulder where Laith was shaking his head. "Keep your voice down." He grabbed his phone. "What part of private are you missing?"

She stepped closer and cupped his crotch. "I've missed this private part. Let's go upstairs and lock the door."

"No, Lexi. I'm in the middle of something."

"You can be in the middle of me." She tugged his arm.

Chapter Thirteen

Sibba stared at her phone like it might bite her. She wasn't sure what had just happened, but it was probably best she didn't. She gave it to Finlee. "If Nash calls, will you answer and tell him I can't talk?"

"Why?" Finlee slid the phone in her back pocket.

"Because I don't wanna talk."

"What's up?"

"Nothing. I just shouldn't have kissed him back. I shouldn't have liked it."

"Damn, girl, you're a red-blooded Southern female, I'd be afraid if you didn't like it. Don't take it so seriously; it was just a kiss."

A kiss that melted my heart and caused a beehive swarm in my stomach. "Yeah, you're right. Just a kiss. Nothing special." Sibba shrugged it off.

They weren't going back to their trailer that night after all because Finlee's Uncle Bart was throwing a big party.

Sibba had loved his parties in high school because she and Finlee would spend the night and stay up late. He had a big warehouse for storing farm equipment. He'd clear it out and set up a sound system to pump country music into the night air. A lot of adults normally came, and some of them offered to be designated drivers. One of the retired bus drivers had a fifteen-passenger van, plus the advantage of knowing where everyone in the county lived.

Sibba enjoyed seeing old friends. Booze flowed freely, as well as other substances which were kept out of sight, but she drank only water. She was proud of her willpower to stay clean, even if she was extremely tempted to take a walk with some friends who blazed.

Finlee stumbled toward her with a phone in her hand. "It's a 'mergency." She collapsed on a bale of hay next to Sibba.

She took the phone. "Nash, what's wrong?"

"I miss you." He slurred worse than Finlee. "I need to see you right away, see-mom girl." He started singing something, but Sibba was damned if she could make it out.

"Are you hurt?"

"If I say yes, will you come?"

"No, but I'll call you an ambulance."

"Come see me, Sibba. Please." The pleading in his voice was more than she could take. "If you don't, I'll find some keys and come see you."

That wouldn't be safe for anyone.

"Just wait till tomorrow. When you wake up,

you won't miss me so much."

"Will too. Okay, I'm going to get keys."

"I don't have a car, Nash."

"I'll come get you. Where are you?"

"Don't. Stay where you are. I'll find some wheels. Steal 'em if I have to. I'm on my way."

He laughed. "You're so funny. That's why I love you."

Sibba stopped mid-stride. "You what?"

He was silent for a moment before he snickered. "You heard me."

"I'll be there shortly. Don't attempt to drive anywhere." She found Uncle Bart and asked for the keys to his truck. He was happy to give them to her, along with a joint.

After tucking the weed into his glove compartment, so he could find it later, she started the engine. She couldn't remember ever driving a dually, but it seemed like a good time to start. Nash had said he loved her.

***

Sibba drove past Nash's fraternity house and parked on the street. The Greek Village reminded her of an ant bed that had been disturbed. She made her way to the front door of the house and bumped into Laith.

He put his arm around her. "There she is. Hey, you. Did you bring me some something, something?"

"Huh?"

"Finlee. She's my little something, something." The beer in his cup sloshed over the side.

"I don't know what that means, but it doesn't

sound nice, and no, I didn't bring her."

"Aww, girl, you know she got it going on. So do you." His hand squeezed her shoulder.

She stepped out of his grasp. "Where's Nash?"

"Ah," he looked around, "try our room upstairs. Third, no…" He counted on his fingers. "Yeah, third door on the left."

Sibba zigzagged between the party-goers to get upstairs. At the appointed door, she knocked. There was no answer. She tried the handle, and it opened to a dark room. Once she flipped the light on, she could see it was the right room because Nash's book bag was on one of the beds. No one was there, but the silence of the space was welcoming, so she stepped in, closing the door behind her.

At the desk by Nash's bed, she picked up a framed photo of him and his brother. She had no doubt Chad was the other boy in the picture because they looked enough alike to be twins. They were young and scrawny. Both of their faces were bright with laughter. She replaced the frame and something sticking out of the desk drawer caught her eye. Being a neat-nick, Sibba couldn't leave it.

She opened the drawer, and the bottom of her heart fell out. With a huff, she slammed the drawer. He was supposed to be getting clean, but he'd called her drunk and the cache of pills told another story.

***

Nash took both of Lexi's wrists in one hand and rolled over on top of her. "I told you no. I'm interested in someone else."

"Come on, she doesn't have to know."

"I didn't try to get with you when you were

72

seeing someone. Why are you trying to ruin what I've started?"

"Because I want you. We're good together." She was drunk and heartbroken, not a good combo.

Nash was losing his buzz and growing impatient with Lexi. Concerned because Sibba hadn't arrived yet, he contemplated calling a cab to go look for her. He hadn't been serious when he said he'd get keys and drive. He was playing dirty to get her to come see him. If he could get her there, Lexi would back off. He hadn't meant to say he loved her, but now that it was out there, he wasn't going to take it back. He'd been trying to deny the fall, but she was someone he wanted a relationship and a future with.

Lexi had lured him into Jon-Jon's room using the excuse she needed to find a picture, but as soon as she'd shut and locked the door, he knew he was in trouble. Her black dress was on the floor, and she'd done a number on his shirt buttons. He wondered if he was making a mistake by putting off a sure thing for uncertainty with Sibba.

Had to be the beer talking.

What if Sibba didn't even like him that way? But the kiss they'd shared that morning said she did.

Someone pounded on the door, and he bolted off the bed to open it.

Dave, the room's occupant, stood there with red rimmed eyes. "Am I at the wrong door?"

"No, come in."

"Nash," Lexi shrieked, "I'm not dressed."

As soon as she said it, Sibba scooted past the door, her eyes narrowed on him. Nash sidestepped

73

Dave, walking fast to catch her, but she maneuvered through the crowds and got away from him. He ran onto the front lawn, looking for the person moving the fastest away from the house. She was halfway down the street. Like a shot, he took off after her and heard Lexi call his name. He glanced over his shoulder to see her chasing him. He ran faster.

Sibba climbed up into a huge truck, and he opened the passenger door, jumping in. He reached for her, but she shoved him away.

"Get out." She cranked the engine.

"Nash." Lexi climbed into the truck next to him. "Why are you running like a crazy person?"

"Why are you chasing me like a crazy person? I told you I'm not interested."

"You can't mean that. I mean, look at me."

He didn't look at her. Instead, he watched Sibba grind her teeth. She looked like she was deciding if she was going to drive off with them in the truck.

"This is the girl I told you about." He reached for Sibba.

She jerked her hand away. "Get out."

"Her? She looks like a hairball my cat coughed up. And look at her clothes. Hippies are so 1970."

Sibba dropped her head in her hands, and Nash turned in his seat to spit venom.

"At least there's nothing fake about her, which is more than I can say for you. She doesn't have to hurl insults to make herself feel superior because she is superior to you in every way. This thing we had, it's over."

"We'll see about that." Lexi nearly fell out of

the truck.

Before he could stop himself, Nash reached to help her and then felt like an idiot for trying. He shut the door when she was gone and turned back to Sibba. "I'm really sorry about her."

"Yeah, well, get the hell out. I'm tired and I'm going home."

"I'm going with you." He buckled his seatbelt.

"No, you're not." She reached across the expanse of seat to unfasten it, and he pulled her into his arms.

She squirmed. "Let me go. I don't want to see you right now." Her voice choked.

He released her. "But you stole a truck and drove all this way to see me."

"That's when I thought…" She slid back behind the wheel and stared straight ahead. "That's before I found out some things about you I don't like."

"Nothing happened with Lexi, so that can't be one of them."

She pushed her glasses up on her hair and rubbed her eyes. "It's been a long day, Nash. Can we talk tomorrow?"

"Yes, we can, but I'm still going with you." He crossed his arms.

Chapter Fourteen

Sibba pulled her pillow over her head when the sun's first rays shone through the window. It had been late when she got to Nash's frat house and later still when she got home. Uncle Bart wouldn't be up anytime soon, so she wasn't in a hurry to get his truck back to him.

When an arm wrapped around her, her eyes popped open. "I thought I told you to sleep on the couch."

Nash pulled her closer to his warm body. She both loved and hated it.

"I want to be where you are." He kissed her hair.

Sibba hated wanting him. He wasn't the guy she thought he was, and yet, she couldn't help herself.

Stay strong. It's not the first time a boy has left you disillusioned. You're not weak anymore.

Reaching for the edge of the blanket, a thought

76

hit her. "You're not naked, are you?"

"I can be in about half a second."

She tossed the covers back. "No, thanks."

He held on tighter. "Don't go."

"If you don't want me to pee on you, you'd better let me go."

He relented and a triumphant smile formed on her lips.

When she returned from the bathroom, her phone rang. "Fin, what are you doing up so early?"

"Sibba, it's Uncle Bart. Finlee overdosed."

Every muscle tensed. "W-What?"

"We're not sure exactly what she had, but…"

"But what?" Nash's hands landed on her shoulders. "Uncle Bart…"

"It…it was…a psychotic break. Hallucinations or something. She's in the psych ward."

"I'm on my way." Sibba grabbed clothes and started to change, forgetting Nash, even though his hands were on her.

He turned her to face him and used his thumbs to wipe tears she didn't know were falling from her eyes.

"I've gotta go."

"Take a deep breath and tell me about it while you change." He turned his back.

***

Sibba prayed for Finlee while Nash drove and held her hand. Her best friend had always been the daring one between them. Finlee was the first to try new things and rarely said no to anything, unless Sibba was there to be the voice of reason.

She hadn't been there. She'd let Finlee down.

Sibba glanced at the glove box, wishing for one hit to settle her nerves. Her grip on Nash's hand tightened until his lips landed on her palm. A shiver raced across her skin. She'd never been kissed there, and something about it was more intimate than she expected.

They pulled into the hospital parking lot. Before getting out, she leaned into Nash and kissed him. His lips were hard with surprise for a second before he relaxed, threading his hand through her hair. The way his tongue stroked hers, slow and rhythmic, made her want more of him. All of him.

They might have stayed like that forever had someone not opened the truck door and interrupted them.

"Dad?" Sibba fanned her glasses on her face to diminish the steam. "What are you doing here?"

"Waiting for you." He took her arm. "Come on. Finlee's been screaming your name."

Sibba slid out of the truck, and her dad held onto her.

He stopped, turning to point at Nash. "I'll deal with you later, young man."

"Dad, it wasn't his fault. I kissed him. Could you please not make this more stressful than it already is?"

Her dad crushed her to his chest. "I'm sorry to upset you, honey, but you'll always be my baby, and I don't want boys kissing you. Any boy. Ever."

Sibba laughed despite herself and hugged her dad back. "Let's go see about Finlee."

When they turned for the hospital, her dad kept an arm around her, and Nash stepped beside her, taking her hand. It struck her as funny that Nash was bold enough to take on her dad.

Sibba always knew the man in her life would have to be strong not to be intimidated by Chief Phil Douglas, which is why she thought she'd have to leave the state of Alabama to find him.

***

Nash waited with Sibba's dad while she went back to see Finlee. "Mr. Douglas, do they know what caused it?"

"Molly laced with bath salts." He narrowed his eyes. "You know what that is?"

"Molly is ecstasy and bath salts is kinda like meth, I think. I never tried it. Heard too many scary things."

"Does my daughter use drugs?"

Nash's face warmed, and his tongue stuck to the roof of his mouth. He shouldn't panic. Her dad would know. Just tell the truth. He cleared his throat. "I've never seen Sibba take a drink, much less do drugs."

Her dad gave him one slow nod as if he were picking apart his words and body language to discern the truth. "Good. Do you use drugs?"

Nash swallowed, and the sound seemed to echo down the corridor. "Only prescription medications."

"Prescribed to you?"

"Phil."

They both turned toward Mrs. Douglas. Nash had met her at Jon-Jon's home. He was struck again by how much Sibba favored her mother. They had the same build and beautiful hazel eyes. The clothes were different though, because Mrs. Douglas wore a

Sunday dress.

Nash let out a long breath, thankful for the interruption. It had almost been a moment of truth. He would've known what he was really made of if he could have told the truth about his drug use. Or, he could just quit. For good.

Taking mid-terms while mourning Jon-Jon's death was more than he wanted to tackle without the help of the pills he was accustomed to. But he wasn't addicted. He could quit. He would quit. And the sooner, the better.

"Mary, this is Sibba's friend and study buddy who doesn't date, but doesn't mind making out with our daughter in a hospital parking lot on a Sunday morning."

Heat spread from Nash's neck up to his face.

Mrs. Douglas tilted her head before she extended her hand. "We've met. You spoke very eloquently at the funeral. I know John and Vera appreciated it."

"Thank you." He dropped his gaze.

"You and Sibba have been spending a lot of time together."

"He doesn't want to date her, but he wants to take her to a dance." One of the Chief's eyebrows was way higher than the other. *That couldn't be good.*

"I see." Mrs. Douglas tried to hide her smile. "And what did she say to the invitation."

"I haven't asked her yet. Things have gone from bad to worse."

"Yes, they have. And it's all your fault."

Nash looked around her parents to see Sibba.

He took a step toward her, but she embraced her mom. His stomach settled in his throat as his mind raced, trying to figure out his part in Finlee's situation.

"What do you mean it's his fault?" her dad asked.

"If he hadn't called me last night and threatened to drive drunk, I wouldn't have left Finlee and she wouldn't be here." She turned her attention to Nash. "I want you to go."

"Is it true? You were drunk last night?" Both eyebrows reached for the ceiling.

Not good.

"Yes, but I…" He took a step toward Sibba, but her dad blocked his way. "Sibba, I'm so sorry."

"Please go."

Her dad grabbed him by the back of his shirt. "Come on, kid."

Nash wanted to fight, to stay and be heard, but the look in Sibba's eyes left him no hope. She was right.

He was to blame.

***

Sibba cried on her mom's shoulder as she watched an out-of-focus Nash walk away. She hated when she got so angry she cried. Hated that she let Finlee down. Hated drugs and the hold they had on people.

Her mom rubbed her back. "We had a prayer service for Finlee at church this morning. What are the doctors saying?"

Sibba wiped her eyes before unhooking her glasses from where she'd hung them on the front of her shirt. "It'll take more time for the drugs to get out of her system so they can see what the long term damage is. Whether or not she gets back in her right mind…" Her voice broke, and Sibba cried out loud. "Oh, Mama, she'll have to go to a psychiatric facility for treatment."

"Baby, try not to worry. The treatment will help her get better." Her mom used a tissue to dab at the corners of Sibba's eyes.

Sibba tried not to think about being alone at the house she shared with Finlee. Or about Finlee not finishing school with her.

"It was wrong to blame your friend."

"He's not my friend. He's the godson of Dr. Ferguson, who's blackmailing me to help Nash do well on the MCAT."

Her mom held her at arm's length. "What in the world are you talking about?"

Sibba sighed and sat in a chair with worn padding. She told her mom about the pipe.

Her mom's eyes welled with tears. "Sibba, how could you risk your life and your future by using drugs?"

Sibba couldn't answer. It had seemed like harmless fun when they'd started. Now, Jon-Jon was dead, and Finlee was possibly brain damaged. These were the consequences of breaking the rules, the law.

Sibba stayed at the hospital for a few hours until Finlee showed improvement. Her paranoia was better, but they sedated her anyway, so she'd rest.

Sibba's mom tried to convince her to stay with them, but Sibba needed to study. She also didn't want to face her dad because her mom would tell him everything.

A sigh escaped her. He'd probably drug test her himself to see if she was really clean.

When she got home, she'd never felt so alone. Her thoughts echoed in the empty spaces left by her best friend. It was lonely without Finlee. Hollow.

Sibba spread her textbook across the dining table, settling in to work on assignments and read ahead, but she had trouble concentrating, especially when she kept looking at the chair Nash had occupied when he'd been over.

Picking up her phone, she considered sending an apology text. He wouldn't want to talk to her after what she'd said, and in front of her parents. Her dad had probably threatened and scared him half to death.

She sighed, put the phone down, and turned the page in her biochem book.

There was a knock at the door, and a little spring of hope welled in her heart at the thought it might be Nash.

She opened the door with an apology on her lips, which she had to swallow. It got stuck in her throat around the lump of terror lodged there.

Her heart rate kicked into overdrive, and she involuntarily took a step back, leaving room for Reid to step inside and close the door.

***

Nash stared at the ceiling of his room until Laith came in.

"Hey, have you talked to Sibba? I've been trying to reach Finlee all day, but she's avoiding me."

"She's not avoiding you." Nash told him about her situation.

Laith sat on his bed. "Call Sibba, so I can find out the latest."

"She won't take my call." Nash explained what he'd done.

"Ah man, that's bullshit. It ain't your fault. Let's ride over there and see if she's home so I can talk to her."

Nash drove, but insisted he wasn't going in, not unless she invited him. He thought back to earlier when Mr. Douglas had dragged him out of the hospital.

He smiled to himself at what he'd said. "It appears I really do have a drug problem."

Her dad hadn't thought it was very funny. Nash had only said it to distract himself from his heart breaking.

Nash had gotten a little scared when instead of taking him back to school, Mr. Douglas turned onto a back road and took him out to a rural area. He parked by some woods. Nash waited in the car while the chief got out and went to the trunk.

A couple minutes later, Mr. Douglas tapped on the window with the stock of a shotgun. Nash's blood froze in his veins, and he swallowed hard. If her dad wanted to off him and bury him in the woods, no one would ever know.

Nash got out of the car and wiped his hands on his jeans. "You planning to make me pay for hurting Sibba and Finlee?"

"I'm planning to teach you how to shoot like

we talked about yesterday."

"Oh." Nash's heart slowly returned to its normal rhythm.

They didn't talk, except for Mr. Douglas giving Nash instructions. By the time they were finished, they'd gone through a lot of rounds. Nash managed to hit a few of the sporting clays, but he was much better with the pistol on the still targets.

When Mr. Douglas had finally dropped Nash at the fraternity house, he got the nerve to ask, "Why are you helping me?"

"Sibba's upset right now, but she cares about you. And you care about her. I can see that. She'll come around, just give her time." He pulled a card from his pocket. "Meanwhile, look out for her from a distance and call me if you need anything. Stay off the booze and drugs, or I'll arrest you myself."

It helped Nash's confidence to know Mr. Douglas trusted him.

Nash took a deep breath as he neared Sibba and Finlee's trailer. It struck him, not for the first time, how secluded it was. Only five miles from town, but no neighbors in sight. He worried about Sibba being there by herself.

Laith got out and knocked on the door.

Nash grabbed the car handle and nearly leapt out when he saw who answered. It was the old boyfriend. The one who'd hurt Sibba.

Nash wondered for a moment if Sibba had invited him. Maybe she did still have feelings for him. She was too smart for that.

He shook off the idea as he slipped the card from his pocket and dialed her dad.

Chapter Fifteen

Sibba eyed the kitchen drawer where they kept a pistol. Reid had instructed her to stay put when someone knocked on the door. So far, he hadn't done anything threatening. Her palms were damp, so she rubbed them on her legs.

She hadn't moved from her chair since she'd returned to it after he came in. Her plan was for him to realize he was interrupting her studying and go. No such luck.

He'd taken the seat across from her and proceeded to roll a joint. For a split second, she wondered if he had given something to Finlee to hurt her. But Finlee hated Reid with a passion, like she wanted to run over him with her truck kind of passion, so she'd never willingly take anything he offered.

Sibba tried not to let him know how uncomfortable she was. He talked to her like nothing bad had ever happened between them, so she pretended things were normal.

When the visitor came unexpectedly, she'd hoped her dad was checking on her. Reid told her he'd get rid of whoever it was, but she really didn't want to be alone with him. Her chest was tight with anxiety.

She recognized Laith's voice, but Reid told him she was resting. Afraid Laith would take Reid at his word and leave, she got up and went to the door. Reid used his arm to keep her behind him.

"Hey, Laith, come on in." Sibba stood on tiptoes to look over Reid's shoulder.

Reid turned, and with his hands on her waist, pushed her back. "You need to go rest."

Laith used the distraction to come in, and Sibba tried to tell him with her eyes that something was off.

She put her hands on Reid's shoulders. "Laith has been dating Finlee. I need to let him know how she's doing. Why don't you go watch television so he and I can talk?"

He was going to say yes, until Nash came in.

"Sibba, is everything all right?"

She started to pull away from Reid. "I…"

Reid wrapped his arm around her waist and pulled her back against the front of his body. Flashes from the past seared her brain.

Gripping his arm, she tried to loosen it. "Reid, lighten up, please."

He tightened his hold and growled in her ear, forcing hot breath on her face. "Who are these guys coming over uninvited? I don't like it. It's why I didn't want you here by yourself."

She struggled with his arm, but it was like a steel hook. "I told you Laith dates Finlee. That's his roommate."

"Hey man, we're just checking on her." Laith put his palms out.

"You sure? I don't like the way your friend is looking at her."

Nash took a step forward, less cautious than Laith. "Sibba is my friend, and it's been a rough weekend. Maybe you could let her go."

"I'll let her go when I'm good and damn ready. You need to leave."

"I'm not going anywhere until you let her go." Nash took another step.

Sibba struggled to get a good breath and was losing the feeling in her midsection. Fear and anger were competing for top emotion as she was getting handled like a rag doll.

She ran through possible ways to get out of her predicament. With a burst of energy, she bent her knees and pushed up.

***

As soon as the back of Sibba's head hit Reid's nose, Nash took her arms and pulled her from his grasp. He maneuvered her behind him and backed them both into the kitchen, where he opened the drawer, tossed the oven mitt, and got the gun.

He'd been surprised when he'd found it accidentally on a prior visit, but was now glad he'd made the discovery. Holding it down by his side, he waited to see what Reid would do. Laith moved behind Nash and checked on Sibba.

Reid's hands covered his nose and blood

dripped down his arms. "You bitch. You broke my nose again."

Sirens sounded in the distance, and Nash prayed they'd hurry. He didn't want to shoot anyone, but he would if it meant protecting Sibba.

"Shit." Reid started for the door.

Nash raised the gun. "Stay right there."

"What? You gonna shoot me?" He sneered. "For what? She ain't hurt." Reid side-stepped toward the door.

"I won't give you the opportunity to hurt her again. Take another step and I'll shoot you in the kneecap." Nash pulled the hammer back and aimed low. He wasn't good with moving targets, but he'd take his best shot.

A hand rested on his shoulder. "Don't shoot him, Nash."

"You still care about him, Sibba?"

"Hell, no. Here, give me the gun. I'll shoot him my damn self." She held her hand out.

Reid backed up and used the hem of his shirt to catch the blood from his nose. "Whatever you do, don't give her the gun."

Blue lights began dancing around the room through the open front door. Nash placed the gun in the drawer and closed it. Sibba laced her fingers with his and held onto his arm with her other hand.

He wasn't ready to turn his back on the enemy. "You okay?"

"Yes." Her voice was a whisper.

The cops came in with guns drawn, and they all put their hands in the air. When Nash heard Sibba's dad's voice outside, he let out a breath and turned to take her in his arms. She hugged him tight, but he kept his grip loose to counteract the rough way Reid had handled her.

Pulling back, he looked at her face. The lenses of her glasses were splashed with tears, so he removed them and kissed each of her eyelids.

She sighed and rested her forehead on his chest. "I'm sorry for what I said."

He cupped the back of her head and used a finger to lift her chin. "Look at me. Don't be sorry. I shouldn't have tricked you into coming to see me. I'm sorry for that. I'm sorry Finlee got into trouble. I know you feel responsible for what happened to her."

"Like you feel responsible for your brother and Jon-Jon?"

He nodded. "I realize it wasn't truly my fault. They made their own choices. I'm still sad about losing them, but I have to let myself off the hook. Can you do that? Can you let me off the hook for Finlee? Yourself too?"

Tears streamed down her cheeks, and she nodded. A strong hand gripped his shoulder, and he looked over at Mr. Douglas.

Her dad placed his other hand on Sibba's back. "You okay, baby girl?"

She sniffled and reached an arm out to him.

Nash backed away to stand by Laith who'd been trying to explain what had happened to the cops. Laith hadn't known about Reid or his history with Sibba, but he said he knew Sibba was afraid of the guy.

Chapter Sixteen

Sibba tossed and turned that night. Each time she dozed off, she felt Reid's arm around her waist and sat straight up in bed. She'd even left the lamp on because in the dark she imagined him coming out of the closet and choking her in her sleep.

Nash was sleeping on the couch at her dad's insistence. In fact, her dad had wanted to stay himself, but had to get back to work investigating who gave Finlee drugs. He didn't want anyone else to overdose on it.

Sibba thought it was a hopeless case. It was most likely an accidental overdose. Finlee had a lot in her system. So much it scared Sibba, who'd always been afraid of the hard stuff.

Cannabis was as wild as she wanted to get for fear of the dangers posed by the more serious drugs. She didn't think she was addicted because even though she frequently thought about its calming effects, she hadn't made a move to get more. It wasn't worth it to her anymore. Wasn't worth losing her future and hurting the people she loved.

Thinking of people she loved, Nash's handsome face covered in dark ginger stubble filled her head.

Before there was a plan in her mind, she opened her bedroom door and padded down the hall.

Sitting up, the blanket fell around his waist, revealing the hard planes of his chest. "What's wrong?"

"Can't sleep."

He tossed the cover back. "What can I do?"

She was disappointed not to find him naked. "Will you come to bed with me?"

"Of course." He stood and put his arm around her.

Her gaze went down to where the waistband of his shorts peeked out from beneath his jeans, which hung low on his hips. He was warm and hard, causing her primal urges to make themselves known. Heat in her core spread low and the muscles of her pelvic floor—of which she could name every one—contracted and released.

She leaned into him as they walked, wanting his comfort and more. When they got to the bed, she turned to face him, stood on her tiptoes, and kissed him.

He was hesitant at first, but when she put her hands around the back of his neck, he opened up and gave her what she was asking for.

He skimmed her hips with his hands. One moved up her back to wind in her hair, and the other went to the lumbar curve of her spine, pulling her closer.

She lowered her hands down the front of his chest to his hips, then let them graze up his back. He shivered and moaned.

Sibba took that as a good sign. Her only experience had been with Reid, and he'd coaxed her into everything.

When Reid had her from behind during their struggle earlier, it had all come back. That was how he'd always taken her. Even for her first time.

She was ready to replace those memories. And this time, she wanted the man to look her in the face when it happened.

She should probably stop kissing Nash and lay down the ground rules.

***

Nash struggled to catch his breath when Sibba broke the kiss. He was glad she was smart enough to stop things from going further. They were both too vulnerable.

"N-Nash..." She glanced down at his chest before she looked back into his eyes. "I know you don't want to date me, but do you think maybe, just for tonight, we could be like you and that Lexi girl?"

"No." He took a step back and took her hands in his.

Her shoulders dropped. "I know I'm not pretty like her, but I was hoping... We could turn out the light even—"

He put a finger over her lips to halt her words. "You and I could never be like Lexi and me because

93

I never felt about her the way I feel about you."

With her chin down, she cut her eyes up to look at him.

"And there's no comparison between you and her. She's pretty, but you're the most beautiful thing I've ever seen."

She raised her eyebrows. "Really?"

"I've been avoiding you since freshman year because you're so attractive. Other guys think so too, but they're intimidated because you're so smart."

She shoved his chest. "Uh-uh."

He took a section of her hair and let it slip through his fingers. "Yah-huh."

She watched as his hand slipped down her side to rest on her hip. She swallowed. "Can we leave the light on then?"

He smiled because her bold request was spoken in a sheepish tone. He shook his head. "No."

Her forehead wrinkled in confusion.

"We're not going there tonight."

"Why not?"

He skimmed a finger down her face before he rested his hands on her shoulders. "Sibba, you've had a rough day...hell, a rough week. We both have. Let's save it for a special occasion."

"Like when?"

He didn't even have to think about it. "How about Winter Formal?"

She twisted her lips and ducked her head again. "I don't really fit in at things like that."

"You fit with me, and that's all that matters. Will you go with me?"

She smiled tentatively. "I guess."

"Good." He kissed her again. "Now, let's get some sleep. We have class tomorrow."

"It's going to be hard to share a bed and not want to…you know."

"I know." He was glad she felt that way. It would be difficult, but he was going to make their first time something neither of them would forget.

They laid down, she on her back and he on his side.

"So, are we still just friends?" she asked.

"No. You're mine. No other man gets to put his hands on you." He pulled her into his arms. "Except your dad. I'm pretty sure he can take me."

She laughed and winced.

He touched her abdomen lightly. "Are you sore?"

"A little."

Another good reason to wait. He kissed the scar next to her eye. "I'm sorry he hurt you again. It was hard not to shoot him."

"I didn't think you'd ever handled a gun before."

"I hadn't before today." He told her about the shooting lesson.

"Nash, I like you, but I can't be yours if you're still using."

He squeezed his eyes shut. Another reason for them to take it slow.

Chapter Seventeen

Sibba dressed up for the second evening in a row. It'd been a week since they buried Jon-Jon, and Nash had been with her every night. The day before, he'd taken her on a real date—dinner and a movie. Now, she was getting ready for dinner with Dr. Ferguson and his family, and she was nervous as all hell.

She hadn't seen the doctor since the last day she'd interned. She'd broken down and told Nash about the pipe, and he was determined to help her get the letter she needed and try to discover if his Uncle Mike had seen it or not.

She was looking in the full length mirror on her closet door when Nash came up behind her and slid his arms around her.

"Don't be nervous. They're going to love you." He kissed her cheek.

She shuddered and turned in his arms to face him, hating to be approached from behind. "As long as you're with me, I'll be okay."

The kiss moved toward the bed, and Sibba wondered how they'd ever make it another month until Winter Formal. They'd agreed to no kissing near the bed, but there they were. Regretfully, it ended so they could leave.

When they arrived at Dr. Ferguson's house, he and his wife greeted them at the door. To her surprise, they both hugged her.

"I didn't know I was playing cupid when I asked you to tutor Nash." Dr. Ferguson took her hand. "But I definitely approve."

A little of the tension eased from her shoulders. He wouldn't have said it if he believed she was a drug user.

She smiled. "Thank you, Dr. Ferguson."

"Call me Mike."

"And me Sara," his wife said.

"I can't. Mama would spank me. How 'bout Dr. Mike and Miss Sara?"

"Works for me," Dr. Mike said and Miss Sara nodded.

Over dinner, the Fergusons quizzed them about their classes, grades, and future plans.

"Actually, Uncle Mike, I've been looking into psychiatry and clinical psychology. What are your thoughts?"

Sibba had already given her opinion. In her mind, Nash was born to help people with psychological distress. They'd been to visit Finlee every day, and the way he was with her amazed Sibba.

Her best friend was getting better and would be

97

out in time for Winter Formal. Laith had invited Finlee to be his date. They would double, and they had all agreed to an evening of good, clean fun. No drugs or alcohol.

"Sibba, are you still looking at schools up north?" Dr. Mike asked.

"Yes, but," she glanced at Nash, "I'm also looking at the Pacific Northwest." She hesitated because he'd probably think she was a flake.

Nash nudged her with his leg. "Tell him. He'll understand."

"They tend to be more accepting of a holistic approach to medicine—a little East meets West."

"I can absolutely see you embracing that avenue. It's your path, Sibba. Follow where it leads you."

Her breath came out in a whoosh, and Nash put his arm around her. "See?"

Before they left, Dr. Mike pulled her aside and gave her an envelope. "Thank you for helping Nash. I was worried he was on the wrong track, but I'm not anymore. It took you to help him figure out who he is and what he wants in life."

Sibba looked down and smiled. "I think we're figuring it out together."

***

Nash helped Sibba inside her house before he went back to his car to get her surprise. His mom was the queen of shopping and all things fashion, so he'd called her for help and described Sibba's personality and style. He'd also called Sibba's mom to get her size.

The package had arrived that morning. Part of

him couldn't wait to show her. The other part was anxious she wouldn't like it and wouldn't like being told what to wear. He'd already seen it and loved it. His mom was in the process of finding a tie, so he'd match.

He went into the house and put the box on the dining table.

"What's this?"

"Don't be mad, but it's a gift from my mom."

Her eyebrows lifted. "For me?"

Nodding, he held his breath while she removed the lid. She looked inside the box for a long moment before she lifted the dress and held it out. It was tie-dyed with big swatches of green, blue, and yellow. But it was evening length, fitted to the knee and flared below. The bodice was beaded, and the back was open.

She went into her room and stood in front of the mirror, holding the dress to her body. "It's the most beautiful thing I've ever seen. I love it."

Nash smiled, his heart rising higher. "You're going to have all the guys checking you out."

She rolled her eyes. "Let's not exaggerate."

He moved behind her and kissed her neck. "I'm not."

She stepped away and turned to face him. It was the second time in one day he'd been behind her, and she'd squirmed out of his arms. He liked looking at her in the mirror, but she didn't seem to like him hugging her from behind.

A flash of the night Reid manhandled her seared his brain. He'd been behind her. She might be suffering from post-traumatic stress and thinking of that every time he touched her.

Her hand rested on his chest. "Are you okay?"

He blinked as her question drew him from his thoughts. "Ah, yeah. Can we talk?"

"Aren't we talking now?"

"Yes, but…" He took the dress from her, laying it across her bed before he took her hand and led her down the hall to the couch.

She put her hands in her lap, and he noticed they were trembling.

His chest tightened. "What's wrong?"

"If you don't want to take me to Winter Formal or if you don't want to be with me, I wish you'd just tell me. I don't want you here out of a sense of obligation because my dad asked you to look out for me." Her eyes were on her lap.

He took her hands. "Sibba, look at me. I want you. I want to be with you. If you don't go to Winter Formal with me, I'll stay home."

"You can't. You're in charge of it."

"I don't know where this insecurity is coming from. If you want me to go, tell me. Otherwise, let me in." He let out a breath. "In your room, just now, I was remembering what happened with Reid. You don't like it when I hug you from behind."

She dropped her gaze. "It's more than just what happened here." She told him about her only experience with sex and Reid.

Nash had to unclench his teeth before he could speak. He lifted her chin. "I can assure you when we make love, I'll be looking right into your beautiful eyes. If there's anything at all that makes you uncomfortable, tell me. Promise?"

She twisted her lips. "Okay."

"I'm glad we're talking about this. What else do you like or dislike? Since we have a launch date, so to speak, the pressure is on."

She grinned. "Are you afraid of failure to launch?"

He laughed as he tickled her. The laughter ended when their lips met, and the desire which was always between them deepened and transformed.

Chapter Eighteen

Sibba blinked and took a moment to allow the foreign bodies invading her eye sockets to settle. She'd been trying to wear the contacts a little each day to get used to them, but she wanted to surprise Nash, so it hadn't been much. She shoved her glasses into their case, tucking it into her overnight bag.

The day had arrived, and Sibba was surprisingly calm. Of course, she was thinking beyond the dance to the bedroom, what she'd been looking forward to for several long weeks. They'd been stuck on third base, and it wasn't that he didn't please her to a near cardiac event every time, but she was craving more. Her insides turned into a roasted marshmallow at the thought of it.

"Sibba-dibba-doo, will you zip me?"

She smiled at Finlee, glad to have her back and of sound mind.

Sibba and Nash had gone through every nook

and cranny of the house to be sure no drugs or related paraphernalia could be found. And Finlee seemed determined to stay clean. The incident had scared her straight.

Nash had also tossed his stash. He'd been irritable at first, and Sibba thought he should buy stock in Red Bull. Caffeine was his new crutch, but since he was changing his major, he was a lot less stressed.

Sibba zipped up Finlee's dress and squeezed her best friend's shoulders. "I'm so glad you're going."

"You're gonna forget my name and your own by the time this night is over." She wasn't talking about chemically-induced amnesia. Finlee knew all about Nash and Sibba's plans.

"Do you think the entire fraternity knows?"

Finlee shook her head. "As far as Laith knows, you guys have been getting it on for weeks."

"Good, can you imagine if they knew? They'd probably call the room and beat on the door all night long."

They'd moved Winter Formal to a ballroom at the nicest hotel in town, so the attendees could get rooms and stay overnight. There was also a shuttle service for those who weren't planning to stay. They were taking the whole anti-DUI thing seriously.

A knock at the door let them know their dates were there. A limousine waited on the driveway, the first of many surprises.

Nash looked at her for a long moment without saying anything. Her hands started to sweat.

"If the scar's too noticeable, I can—"

He put his lips on hers and let them linger a moment. "You're perfect, scars and all."

Heat crawled up her neck, and he kissed her cheek before he took her bag to the car.

On the ride, Nash poured sparkling cider into champagne flutes for each of them. Laith interlaced his fingers with Finlee's and brought her hand to his lips. Laith was a nice guy, and he had it bad for Finlee. Sibba was glad they'd made a pact to stay clean, for themselves and for her.

Nash's arm slipped around Sibba's shoulders. "You don't seem nervous at all."

"I'm not." She winked.

"That makes one of us."

"Not having performance anxiety, are you?" she whispered in his ear.

He sighed. "Not really. Once we get through the meal and ceremony, I'll be able to relax."

"Is Dave doing any better coping with Jon-Jon's death?"

He shook his head. "Not so much."

"I'm proud of you for doing everything. I know you had help, but I also know with him out of commission, the responsibility fell on you."

"You might be the only person, besides my parents, who has ever said they're proud of me."

She ran her finger down his cheek. "Well, I am."

There was no denying what she saw in his eyes. *Love.* It'd been growing between them practically since they met.

Her heart overflowed, and she couldn't wait to

show him just how much she loved him back.

***

Nash asked Sibba to wait with Finlee and Laith while he took her bag up to their suite. He didn't want her to see it and ruin the surprise. The fraternity had gotten a block of rooms at a discounted rate, but he'd sprung for the honeymoon suite. While it wasn't technically their honeymoon, it kind of was. He'd take her someplace really great for their real honeymoon. Though she didn't know it yet, they were going to get married after graduation, before medical school, if things went according to plan.

The only kink in an otherwise flawless evening of dinner and dancing was Lexi. She'd wrangled an invitation and ignored her date most of the night to pay unwelcome attention to Nash and Sibba.

"I don't have to tell you how good he is in bed, do I?" Lexi licked her lips and stared at his crotch.

It was so *not* sexy.

"No, you don't." Sibba sidled closer to him. "He can make me holler in six languages, and I don't even speak English very well."

Nash covered his mouth with his hand to stifle a laugh.

"I don't suppose you'd share him with me, would you?" Lexi ran a long, fake fingernail down his tie-dyed tie.

"Not a chance, but I *will* snatch you bald-headed if you touch him again."

"Careful, Sib. That could happen more easily than you think, since her hair is mostly extensions," he said.

Lexi slapped him and turned for the bar.

Sibba kissed his stinging cheek. "I'm glad she has extensions. She doesn't deserve hair that perfect."

"No one's hair is as beautiful as yours."

She grunted. "This mop is my bane."

"You know how much I love it and how I can't wait to tangle my fingers in it." He wriggled his eyebrows.

"Why wait?" She bit her lower lip, but her smile blossomed despite her efforts to stop it.

"I'm ready when you are."

She took his hand. "Lead on."

He paused with key in hand outside the door of their room.

Sibba raised an eyebrow in question and waited while he reached for a remote inside his coat pocket. Before he opened the door, he grinned at her and hit play.

Sibba's eyes lit up. "My theme song. You pulled out all the stops."

As Neil Young's "Cinnamon Girl" played, he closed the door and watched her take it all in. He'd left cider chilling in an ice bucket and bouquets of flowers on every flat surface. It was like a scene from a chick flick, but the rose petals leading to the bed was something he did because he wanted her to know she was worth the effort.

She turned and kissed him. When he started maneuvering them toward the bed, she stopped him.

"I need a minute in the bathroom." She took her bag, went in, and closed the door.

He removed his jacket and tie and unbuttoned

his collar and cuffs.

When the door opened, his mouth literally watered. She wore a purple silk tie-dyed nightie, which stopped at the top of her thighs.

He swallowed. "Please tell me you have the panties to match."

She turned to the side and raised the hem slowly. Bare skin greeted him until it was high enough to reveal the thin strap of the barely-there panties. They matched.

"I love you, Sibba Douglas." He closed the space between them and reached in his pocket.

She touched his cheek. "I love you too, Nash Lincoln."

"Good." He slid the ring on her finger.

Epilogue

Sibba had been telling everyone for a year and a half that it was a promise ring, not an engagement ring. Nash was good with it as long as she called it an "I'll promise to marry you one day ring".

They'd already graduated and would be moving to Washington State in a few weeks. She'd gotten into medical school, and he was starting a Ph.D. program there, even though he'd done well on the MCAT after all.

He'd been worried about disappointing his parents, and they'd been worried about him pursuing a dream which wasn't his own.

Finlee had taken a year off from school and had planned to go back, but somehow she went from being a farmer's daughter to a farmer's wife when she married Laith in his senior year. And now, four months later, Sibba learned she was going to be an aunt.

Sibba shook her head at her friend. "You're

supposed to wait until I'm on OB rotation, so I can deliver the little critter."

"I know, I'm sorry." Finlee hugged Sibba tight. "I'm gonna miss you so much. Please move back some day so we can be besties again."

"Again? We aren't gonna stop. You'll always be my best friend."

"Hey, I thought I was your best friend." Nash hugged her from behind, and she didn't even mind.

"You're my other BFF."

"Forever? Do you mean that?" he asked.

Sibba nodded.

"Prove it," he said in her ear.

"All right, I will." She turned to face him, slipping her arms around his waist. "Go on, drag me down the aisle already."

His eyebrows shot up. "Are you serious?"

"Yep."

"Let's do this before I'm too big to fit in a regular dress." Finlee put her hands on her belly.

"Do they make tie-dyed wedding dresses?" Nash asked.

Sibba grinned. "If not, we'll make our own."

ABOUT THE AUTHOR

Meda White is an award-winning author who writes sweet, sultry, and southern contemporary and new adult romance. Born with Georgia clay running through her veins, she continues to enjoy the Southern lifestyle with her husband, a very spoiled Collie, and a stray cat who adopted the family. When not writing, you might find her making music, shooting zombie targets, teaching yoga, or explaining the meaning of her unusual first name.

A Note to Readers

Thank you for reading *Winter Formal*. I hope you enjoyed Sibba and Nash's love story. It was enlightening to research some of today's drugs of choice. If you're interested in the other Southern College Novellas, stay tuned for a sneak peek at *Spring Fling*.

If you have a moment to leave an honest review, I'd really appreciate it. Not only do reviews let authors know how they're doing, they help readers find new books.

I love to hear from readers. Please look for me on my Website, Facebook, Twitter, and my Dirt Road Darlings street team. If you sign up for my Newsletter, which contains bonus material and sometimes prizes, it'll make sure you never miss a new release.

Thank you, and best wishes for a lifetime of love and laughter.

Meda

Spring Fling

Kellyn Crenshaw got up from her poolside chaise lounge in a huff. It was the middle of a warm day during Spring Break of her senior year of college, and she should be buzzed and happy. Instead, she was sick of seeing her drunk best friend, Indi, being the center of male attention. Especially, since Indi had a boyfriend back in Georgia.

Kellyn was growing increasingly jealous of her friend. Not only because the boys described Indi's body as smokin' hot, but because Indi had dark hair and eyes and could turn a pretty shade of tawny when she sat in the sun. Whereas, Kellyn was a red head with green eyes. The only tan she could muster came from a can or a spray booth, but both had left her splotched, streaked, and stinky in the past, so she tried to accept her ghostly state of existence.

If she were honest, she'd always been a little jealous of Indi who was outgoing and made friends easily. Kellyn considered herself lucky to befriend Indi freshman year because she pulled Kellyn out of her shell and helped her meet a lot of people. They'd had a fun four years and this Spring Break was supposed to be their last hoorah.

Kellyn moved away from the crowd and onto the white sands of Panama City Beach, Florida to spray another layer of SPF 7000 onto her exposed skin. Indi had talked her into the black bikini, and while Kellyn thought it looked okay, it left too much skin to be burned by the sun's harmful rays.

"I'll get your back." Pace Samson approached with his hand out.

"Thanks." She passed the bottle to him and pulled her hair to the side. Her ponytail was sticking through the hole in her baseball cap, but it was so long it would get sprayed if she didn't move it.

She jumped when the cold spray hit her back, and Pace laughed at her. He loved to laugh and joke and could find humor in most situations. They had become sort of friends since Indi started dating his roommate and best friend, Cobie. But, Kellyn didn't care for the rate at which Pace went through women. He did it faster than some guys changed underwear. Some of her sorority sisters had been left brokenhearted by *Pace who leaves without a trace.*

Indi and Cobie had been dating since Winter Formal, so Kellyn was over at Cobie and Pace's apartment more often than she cared to admit. She didn't have anything better to do and the guys were entertaining. It was even a little funny the way Pace would thrust his hips in a lewd gesture and joke about his conquests. Kellyn promised herself she would never be one of them.

"Do you think I need some of this? I'm not getting too much sun, am I?" He held his hands out and did a slow turn for her.

He had all-American good looks—light brown hair, mischievous blue eyes, and muscles. Many of the fraternity boys had beer guts, but Pace carried a six pack out in front.

Kellyn tried to focus on his skin, instead of his muscles. "Your shoulders look a little pink."

113

"Hit me."

She smirked at the thought of smacking him upside the head, but instead pressed the nozzle of the sunscreen. The wind caught it and blew it back in her face. She coughed and made gagging noises, trying to get the taste out of her mouth.

"Are you all right?" He barely contained his laughter.

"Yeah." She pushed his back. "Turn this way." She managed to get it on his shoulders then.

"Rub it in."

"You don't have to; that's the point of the spray."

"I know, but sometimes it doesn't get evenly distributed. For all I know, you could be writing '*Player*' across my shoulders."

"I wish I would've thought of that. It could be a Public Service Announcement to warn the unsuspecting ladies, but I'm typically not that mean."

"You're pretty mean to me."

She put the can between her knees and reached up to rub the SPF into his skin. "You deserve it. You have boyfriend potential, but your track record sucks. You treat girls like meat."

Also Available from Meda White

Spring Fling
A Southern College Novella

Kellyn Crenshaw wants to make it to college graduation without becoming another notch on the belt of a fraternity boy. A boy exactly like Pace Samson. Forced into close proximity because their roommates are dating, Kellyn sets out to prove she's resistant to his charms.

Pace never figured himself for a one-woman man until he spends time with Kellyn. She's different, and he can't get her out of his mind. She's also aware of his reputation, and it may keep him from the one girl who makes him want to change his ways.

When Pace and Kellyn fake a fling on Spring Break to help their friends, Kellyn may discover she isn't immune to Pace after all. They'll each have to decide if what's between them is just a fling or if there's a chance their feelings are real.

Fall Rush
A Southern College Novella

Embry Harris is desperate to turn things around her senior year of college. She's determined to make more responsible choices and rid herself of the stigma plaguing her. But because of her job and the hot bartender who goads her into making impulsive decisions, it isn't going to be easy.

Stede Bennett's mission since returning from his overseas tour is to get his degree. The last thing he needs is a spoiled sorority girl distracting him. Being a Marine taught him many things, except how to handle a beautiful woman in constant need of saving.

Protecting Embry from the jerk threatening to ruin her reputation is how Stede begins to lose his heart. Being empowered by Stede's words is how Embry starts losing hers. If the schemer responsible for pushing them together gets his way, they could lose their chance for happiness.

Christmas Give
A Holiday Novella

Eva Walker returns home to Georgia for the first Christmas since her husband's death. She's missed her family, but is afraid the void left by her husband will make it unbearable.

Between losing his job as an NFL defensive back and losing his wife to the star quarterback, Adam "Mack" Riggs has had a rough year. Looking for a change of pace, he visits an old college friend for Christmas.

The attraction between Eva and Adam is instant, and so is the laughter. Enjoying life again feels so good for both of them. Simple Christmas wishes unite with a shared holiday tradition, putting them on a path toward healing and acceptance. A path that could lead to a future, if only their pasts would remain where they belong.

Play With My Heart
A Southland Romance Book 1

Southern musician and closet geek Liz Baker enjoys her quiet life. While in Los Angeles helping her brother with a house project, the simple life gets complicated when British television actor Ian Clarke walks into the picture.

Ian enjoys his celebrity status in Hollywood and is determined nothing and no one will get in the way of his plans for success on the big screen. He never counted on meeting a woman like Liz, but she's the only one who can help him with a personal problem.

Forced into close quarters where priorities and cultures clash, an intense attraction catches them both by surprise. Secrets, old lovers and the paparazzi threaten their new dreams and a chance for love could be lost forever.

***Play With My Heart* is the 2014 BTS Red Carpet Award Winner in Contemporary Romance**.

Dance With My Heart: A Southland Romance Book 2
Ride With My Heart: A Southland Romance Book 3
Fool With My Heart: A Southland Romance Book 4